Whispers of the Silent Mind

Reflections on Life's Bonds

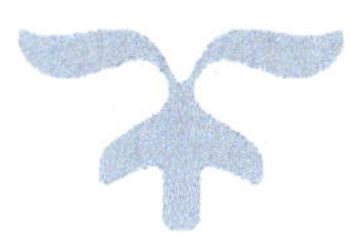

VIJAY KUMAR PUCHA

Dedicated

To my Parents

To my parents

Whose wisdom, sacrifices, and guidance have shaped me into
who I am today.

To my brothers and sister.

For standing by me, sharing both burdens and joys and being my
constant source of strength.

To my wife and children

Your patience, love, and belief in me have been my greatest
motivation. You are the reason I strive for more.

To my mentors

For your endless love, unwavering support, and the strength
you've given me throughout this journey.

And to all those who have walked with me,

Whether through the brightest moments or the darkest hours.

this book is for you.

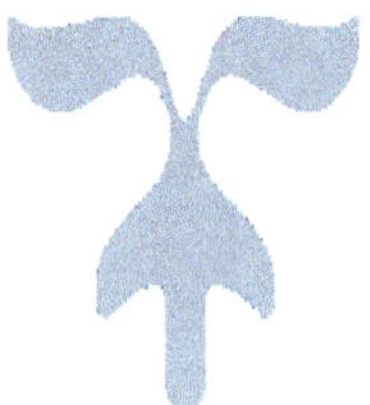

Acknowledgments

I wish to extend my heartfelt thanks to the previous generation, whose wisdom and support have profoundly shaped my life. The lessons they imparted and the roles they played have become an integral part of who I am today. Their influence is woven into the very fabric of my understanding and growth.

> Many Putchas' have come and gone,
> Generations pass as time moves on,
> In the swift march of days, we remain,
> Survivors of a lineage, through joy and pain.

I would like to express my deepest gratitude to my father, Sri Rama Murthy Putcha, who passed away in February 2024. As a guardian, a scholar, and with a keen interest in literature, he has been a guiding influence on generations of Putchas. His wisdom and love for knowledge continue to inspire us all.

I also wish to thank my late father-in-law, Sharad Chandra Kulkarni, a retired schoolteacher from Panhala Vidya Mandir in Panhala, Maharashtra. Though he passed away a few years ago, his wish to see this book completed has been a guiding light throughout this journey.

I am also deeply appreciative of the present-day support that has guided me. These contributions—from the past and present—have enriched my journey and continue to inspire my work. Writing is enriched through collaboration, where feedback and editing enhance the work. Books are judged on quality and impact, but an author's worth transcends any single work. Embracing feedback fosters growth and broadens creative possibilities.

Lastly, I would like to acknowledge modern technology for its invaluable guidance and insightful contributions throughout the development of this work. While its role has been significant, the creation and expression of these ideas remain a testament to my own creativity and dedication.

In tribute to the inspirations that have guided this journey, the poetic titles reflect the themes and emotions that permeate the works:

"Whispers of the Silent Mind"

In the quiet corners where thoughts reside,
Whispers linger, and secrets hide,
An echo from a mind serene,
Unveils the truths that the heart has seen.

"Whispers of the Silent Mind is a beautiful collection of lessons well crafted in poems that are easy to read and Reflections that convey clearly the lessons the son's father spent his lifetime imparting. I highly recommend this book to anyone who has an interest in anything spiritual and anyone wishing to live their life to the fullest."

Pam Collings, Editor, TB Books

Book Introduction:
Whispers of Wisdom:
A Journey Through Generations

Whispers of Wisdom: A Journey Through Generations is a reflective and deeply personal exploration of life's most profound lessons, as experienced by a son through the wisdom imparted by his father. Each chapter delves into universal themes—love, success, humility, perseverance, and the intricate dance of relationships—that resonate across generations. Through a blend of prose and poetry, the book captures the essence of the father's teachings, offering timeless insights that guide the son as he navigates the complexities of his own journey.

The narrative unfolds as the son reflects on various aspects of life, from the importance of staying true to one's path to the value of silent perseverance. The father's wisdom serves as a guiding star, illuminating the way forward in both moments of triumph and times of struggle. Each chapter is a vignette, offering a glimpse into the intimate exchanges between father and son, where the father's quiet strength and profound understanding shape the son's worldview.

The book emphasizes the importance of embracing change, understanding the fluidity of roles, and finding balance in a world that is often chaotic and unpredictable. It speaks to the challenges of modern life while grounding its lessons in the enduring values of family, integrity, and self-discovery.

Through the pages of this book, readers are invited to reflect on their own journeys, to find comfort in the shared human experience, and to discover the quiet power that lies in wisdom passed down from one generation to the next. *Whispers of Wisdom* is not just a collection of reflections; it is a celebration of the timeless bond between father and son, and the lasting impact of the lessons that shape our lives.

Contents

The Hidden Pages - 1

In the quiet of his father's room,
Where dust had settled like a silent plume,
The son explored with careful hands,
The remnants of life's shifting sands.

Among the clothes and faded tomes,
He found a book, its cover worn,
No title graced its aged face,
Yet within, he found a hidden grace.

Pages turned with gentle care,
Thoughts scribbled here; reflections rare.
Some verses flowed with rhythmic beat,
Others, fragments, incomplete.

What could a life of seeming strife,
Hold in its depths, devoid of prize?
Yet as he read, a truth unfurled,
In quiet words, a richer world.

A man not famed, nor rich, nor known,
Had left a legacy of thought alone.
In every line, a glimpse revealed,
A soul's true essence, deeply sealed.

The son absorbed each tender line,
Finding depth in simple rhyme.
Through these unspoken, heartfelt streams,
He saw his father's quiet dreams.

Thus, in the pages worn and thin,
He found the man beneath the skin,
And through his thoughts, was forged a bond,
A legacy of love, nourished from beyond.

Reflection 1: The Hidden Pages

As the days passed, the son continued his quiet exploration of his father's room, piecing together fragments of a life that had been lived with quiet dignity and understated strength. The room was not just a collection of objects; it was a mosaic of memories, each item telling a part of the story. But the son soon realised that the true essence of his father's life extended beyond these four walls.

His thoughts turned to the people who had been a part of his father's world—the relatives and friends who had walked alongside him through the ups and downs of life. These relationships had been a cornerstone of his father's existence, providing both support and a sense of belonging. The son remembered the countless family gatherings, the shared meals, and the stories that were passed around like treasured heirlooms. It dawned on him that these people weren't just a part of his father's life; they were a part of his own story, too.

In the quiet moments of reflection, the son began to understand the importance of these connections. They were more than just blood ties; they were the keepers of shared experiences, the walking memories of a life well-lived. His father had always valued these relationships, understanding that they held the threads of continuity that linked the past with the present. Severing these ties would mean losing a part of oneself, a part of the shared history that made life meaningful.

The True Measure - 2

I don't compete with you, my fight's not here,
There's nothing to prove, no challenge near.
My struggle aligns with one who knows,
The path we walked, where hardship grows.

Your father and I began this race,
With equal time and shared embrace.
The same resources, teachings, pain,
Together we withstood the strain.

You are the fruit of battles fought,
Born with all the ease we sought.
You stand on ground we carved with might,
But you've not faced our darkest night.

So, if you wish to understand,
Come down, start fresh, and take my hand.
Or stay aside, for you don't see,
The war that's waged inside of me.

The measure's not in what you hold,
But in the stories left untold.
The real contest lies in the past,
With those who faced the storm, steadfast.

Reflection 2: The True Measure

The son's journey through his father's life wasn't just about uncovering physical objects; it was also about rediscovering the values and lessons that had been subtly woven into the fabric of his upbringing. One memory, in particular, stood out—a day when a neighbour's son, freshly successful and full of youthful pride, came by to visit. He was eager to show off his achievements and to prove how bright and capable he was, especially in comparison to the older, more experienced generation.

The son remembered how his father listened patiently, his face calm and thoughtful. When the young man was finished, his father didn't respond with envy or criticism. Instead, he offered a quiet, measured response that spoke volumes about the wisdom he had gained through years of hard-earned experience. It was a lesson the son would only fully appreciate later in life—a lesson about humility, the value of perseverance, and the true measure of a person's worth.

The son could still hear his father's words echoing in his mind, not as a rebuke but as a reminder of what truly mattered. His father had seen the world differently, understanding that life wasn't about competing with others but about facing one's own challenges with dignity and strength. It wasn't about what you achieved in comparison to others; it was about the stories and struggles that shaped you.

The Stages of Our Time - 3

Son, we walk through time's embrace,
In stages marked by life's own pace.
The first is where experience grows,
In every step, new wisdom flows.

We start with eyes so fresh and bright,
Learning life's truths, both day and night.
These early days, we gather much,
In every word, in every touch.

Then comes the stage where we mature,
Where all we've learned begins to blur,
Into patterns, clear and strong,
We find the place where we belong.

The stage of learning never fades,
It shifts and grows, in different shades.
We seek the knowledge deep and wide,
To understand, to turn the tide.

Next, we teach what we've amassed,
Guiding others with lessons passed.
Our wisdom is shared, in quiet ways,
A beacon through life's winding maze.

And in these steps, our wisdom's born,
Through nights of doubt, through every morn.
It's not just knowing but learning to see,
The depth of life's vast complexity.

Then comes the time to give and sow,
To plant the seeds, to watch them grow.
Contribution, our gift to earth,
To leave behind a trace of worth.

Finally, we reap what we have sown,
In this stage, we're not alone.
We reflect on all that we have done,
The battles fought, the races won.

These stages, son, are life's own way,
To shape our journey, day by day.
Embrace each one, let none be missed,
For in them all, life's truth persists.

Reflection 3: The Stages of Our Time

As the son continued to reflect on the lessons his father had taught him, he realised that his father's wisdom wasn't just about specific moments or events. It was about understanding the broader journey of life—the stages that each person goes through and the importance of embracing each one with grace and awareness. He remembered a particular conversation where his father had taken the time to explain these stages, not as rigid steps but as fluid phases that everyone experiences in their own way.

His father had spoken about how life begins with a thirst for knowledge and experience, a time when everything is new and full of potential. He explained how, as we grow, the lessons we learn start to take shape, influencing our decisions and guiding our paths. But learning never truly stops; it evolves, deepening our understanding of the world and our place within it.

His father had also emphasised the importance of passing on what we've learned, of becoming teachers and guides for others. This, he said, was one of life's greatest responsibilities—to share wisdom, to help others navigate the complexities of life. And finally, his father had spoken of reflection, of looking back on the life we've lived, not with regret, but with a sense of fulfilment, knowing that we've contributed something meaningful to the world.

These stages, his father had told him, were the framework of a life well-lived. The son, now older and wiser himself, saw the truth in these words. He understood that each stage was not an end but part of a continuous journey, one that required both strength and humility.

The Invisible Thread - 4

The girls in the family are a treasured wealth,
Their laughter and grace, a source of health.
When they find a man, a sweet new bond,
Their hearts entwine, in love so fond.

A daughter walks her way through life,
Creating worlds, becoming a wife.
Or adjusting gently, as life demands,
Building homes with her tender hands.

Brothers stand with a silent vow,
To protect and guide, no matter how.
Through the years and every shade,
They promise to guard until they fade.

The bonds of love form an invisible thread,
Veins unseen, yet the blood is fed.
Connections strong, though out of sight,
They hold us close through the darkest night.

For family ties are woven deep,
In every heart, their secrets keep.
Though miles apart or lives may change,
The love remains, unbound by range.

So cherish these bonds, these threads of gold,
For in their weave, true love is told.
And as the daughters find their way,
The blood of kin will never sway.

Reflection 4: The Invisible Thread

The son's exploration of his father's life led him to think deeply about the relationships that had been woven into the fabric of his own existence. His father had always emphasised the importance of family and friends, not just as companions in life but as integral parts of one's identity. These connections, his father had explained, were like threads in a vast tapestry, each one contributing to the overall.

As I reflected on my father's words, I began to see how deeply intertwined our lives are, even when distance separates us. The bonds we share are not merely of blood but of shared experiences, of moments that linger in our hearts long after they have passed.

He often spoke about how love and relationships are like an invisible thread—strong, unbreakable, yet delicate in their own way. It's not something we always see, but we feel it in the moments of silence, in the unspoken understanding between people who truly care for one another.

As time moves forward, I realize that relationships evolve. The laughter of childhood gives way to the wisdom of adulthood. The roles shift, but the connection remains, adapting to the ever-changing tides of life. My father's love, his guidance, and his lessons are still with me, even though he is no longer here in person.

The invisible thread that binds us is woven from trust, shared history, and an unspoken promise to carry forward the values we've inherited. It is in the way we remember, in the lessons we pass on, and in the love that continues to guide us, even from afar.

In the Challenging Days - 5

In the challenging days, families fight,
Seeking solace in the fading light.
Their hearts in turmoil, their spirits torn,
Looking to each other, weary and worn.

They search for help, for hands to hold,
For words of comfort, for love untold.
And they gather close, hearts filled with care,
To shelter each other, to be there.

They give all they can, their very best,
To ease the pain, to grant some rest.
In every tear, in every plea,
They offer their strength, their love's decree.

For when the storm clouds gather near,
And their eyes are filled with growing fear,
The family stands as a fortress strong,
A haven where they all belong.

They give their all, they do not sway,
In the hope that soon, the storm will lay.
Their love a beacon in the night,
Guiding them all through the fight.

And though the days may bring more strife,
A family's love is a guiding light.
For in their hearts, a vow is made,
To keep each other safe, and unafraid.

Reflection 5: In the Challenging Days

As the son continued to reflect on the life lessons his father had imparted, he found himself thinking about the difficult times they had faced as a family. His father had always been a pillar of strength during these moments, guiding the family through challenges with a calm and steady hand. But it wasn't just his father's strength that had seen them through—it was the collective resilience of the family, bound together by love and mutual support.

He remembered a particularly tough period when everything seemed to be going wrong. The family was tested in ways they had never imagined, and it was easy to feel overwhelmed. But his father had a way of making them all feel safe, even when the world outside was uncertain. He didn't just offer words of comfort; he showed them, through his actions, what it meant to stand firm in the face of adversity.

His father had taught him that difficult times were an inevitable part of life, but they were also opportunities to grow stronger, both as individuals and as a family. It was during these bad days that the true nature of their bonds was revealed. They learned to rely on each other, to find strength in unity, and to never lose hope, no matter how bleak things seemed.

Now, looking back, the son could see how those tough times had forged an unbreakable bond within the family. They had emerged from the storm not just intact but stronger, more united, and with a deeper appreciation for each other.

The Brides Who Walk In - 6

Brides join a family with their gentle grace,
Hoping to find a familiar place.
They look for the same warmth, the same light,
In a world that's new, in a home so bright.

They step into lives they barely know,
With hearts full of hope, ready to show,
Support for a team they've yet to see,
Values unclear, yet they long to be.

Familiar faces are few and far,
Yet they stand tall, like a guiding star.
With courage and strength, they begin to weave,
A bond with strangers, a world to believe.

These girls who come in with so much to give,
Their potential shines in the way they live.
They learn, they grow, they adapt with grace,
In unfamiliar hands, they find their place.

For every bride who steps into the unknown,
A new chapter starts, a seed is sown.
And though the path may seem unsure,
Their spirit endures, their hearts secure.

In time, the unfamiliar becomes dear,
The values take shape, the love grows near.
And these brides, with potential so grand,
Build a new world with their own hand.

Reflection 6: The Brides Who Walk In

The son's reflections on his father's life naturally led him to think about transitions and new beginnings. He remembered the stories his father had told him about the women in their family, especially the brides who had entered the family over the years. Each one had come into a new world, often leaving behind everything familiar to start a life with people they barely knew.

His father had a deep respect for these women, understanding the courage it took to embrace such profound change. The son recalled his father saying that a bride didn't just join a family; she helped to shape it, bringing with her new traditions, values, and a fresh perspective. This transition wasn't always easy, but it was essential for the growth and continuity of the family.

The son now saw how these new beginnings had enriched the family, how each bride had woven her own story into the larger tapestry of their shared history. These women had not only adapted to their new lives but had also contributed to the strength and resilience of the family. They had forged bonds that would last a lifetime, creating a sense of unity that was both strong and tender.

As the son thought about the future, he realised that every new beginning, no matter how challenging, held the potential for growth and transformation. His father had taught him that it was not just the destination that mattered, but the journey itself and the people who walked beside you along the way.

The Brand of Being - 7

Everything is named; each has its brand,
Qualities etched by an unseen hand.
Behaviors observed, with patterns aligned,
Even the stars in their paths defined.

The planets and stars, they're given their names,
Their influence noted, their roles in the games.
They say these forces will mold and will shift,
Change your essence, give you a lift.

Be wary, my son, of the world's silent song,
For you are refined by what's right and wrong.
Each day, a chisel, a subtle design,
Carves your soul in ways so divine.

Qualities built upon you take form,
Even if you resist, even if you scorn.
You are named, and with that name,
A brand is forged, a lasting claim.

You may wish to ignore, to cast it aside,
But this mark will stay; there's nowhere to hide.
For in your features, in all that you do,
The world has stamped its impression on you.

Yet in this branding, there lies a great choice,
To find your own strength, to lift up your voice.
For though they name you, though they confine,
You hold the power to truly define.

So wear your brand, but know its true worth,
You are more than labels assigned at your birth.
In every name, in every trait,
Lies the chance to create your own fate.

Reflection 7: The Brand of Being

As the son delved deeper into his father's writings and memories, he began to think about the concept of identity. His father had often spoken about how a person's identity is shaped—not just by their own choices but by the names, labels, and expectations placed upon them by others. Yet, his father had also taught him that while these external forces could influence who we become, they do not have to define us.

The son remembered how his father would sometimes speak about the struggle to maintain one's true self in a world that constantly tries to mould you into something else. He understood now that his father had navigated this struggle with quiet strength, choosing to define himself on his own terms despite the pressures around him. It wasn't always easy, but it was a journey his father believed was worth taking.

His father's words echoed in his mind: "You may be named, you may be branded, but the power to redefine yourself always lies within you." The son realised that identity was not a static thing; it was something that evolved, something that could be reclaimed and reshaped as one grew and learned. His father's life was a testament to this belief, and it was a lesson the son knew he would carry with him always.

The Stars and the Heart - 8

Some run around, predicting the skies,
Reading the future where the planets lie.
They trace the paths, the cosmic play,
And tell you what the stars might say.

But look into your heart, find what you seek,
For in its depths, your true desires speak.
Work as hard as you can, give it your all,
Build your dreams, stand proud and tall.

Then leave the rest to the stars above,
For they may guide, but it's you who must love.
Don't build your castle on shifting sands,
Or by the light of another's hands.

For the stars may twinkle, they may shine,
But it's your heart that draws the line.
In its beat, your destiny is found,
So don't turn your castle the other way around.

Trust in yourself, let your dreams take flight,
And the stars will bless you with their light.
But remember, it's you who must lead the way,
Through the darkest night and the brightest day.

Reflection 8: The Stars and the Heart

The son's reflections on his father's wisdom often brought him back to one of the most profound lessons his father had shared—the delicate balance between destiny and free will. His father had always believed that while the stars might influence the course of our lives, it was ultimately the choices we made, guided by the desires of our hearts, that determined our path.

The son recalled late-night conversations where his father would speak of the stars, not as cold, distant objects, but as symbols of the possibilities that lay before each person. He had taught the son to look up at the night sky and see not just a map of fate, but a canvas of opportunities waiting to be seized. His father's view was that life was a dance between what was written in the stars and what was crafted by one's own hands.

The son understood now that his father had always encouraged him to follow his heart, to trust in his own instincts and desires, even when the path seemed uncertain. The stars might offer guidance, but they were not the final word. The son's journey was his own to shape, and his father's quiet confidence in his ability to do so had always been a source of strength.

The Dance of Relationships - 9

The planets are called in a strange, wise way,
Each with a power, a role to play.
In the cosmic dance, they take their place,
Guiding our lives through time and space.

Saturn, like elders with wisdom vast,
A keeper of time, with lessons that last.
It teaches patience, builds our will,
Through trials and tests, we climb the hill.

Mars burns bright like friends who strive,
The fire of action, they keep us alive.
They fuel our passions, ignite the fight,
In every challenge, they give us might.

Jupiter, grand like mentors and guides,
Expands our minds, where wisdom abides.
In its light, our dreams take flight,
Guiding us through the darkest night.

Mercury whispers like neighbours do,
Bringing fresh ideas, perspectives new.
In every exchange, thoughts rearrange,
Guiding our words through life's vast range.

Venus shines like the love we hold dear,
Daughters and sons, those we keep near.
In harmony's sway, they light our way,
Bringing beauty and love into every day.

The Moon reflects like friends so true,
Mirroring our soul, in light's gentle hue.
It ebbs and flows with silent grace,
Revealing truths in its soft embrace.

The Sun stands tall, the family's core,
The source of life, of love and more.
It lights our path, it warms our days,
In its glow, we find our ways.

Together they dance, in celestial rhyme,
Each with a purpose, each with a time.
They shape our fate, they mould our ways,
In their cosmic light, we spend our days.

Reflection 9: The Dance of Relationships

The son had always been fascinated by the way his father spoke of the planets, not just as distant celestial bodies but as symbols of the many relationships that filled their lives. His father believed that just as the planets influence the tides and seasons, so too do the people in our lives shape our experiences, guide our actions, and mould our character.

His father would often draw parallels between the planets and the various roles that people play in a family and community. He would speak of Saturn, with its steady, unwavering presence, as akin to the wise elders in the family—relatives who, with their experiences, teach patience and fortitude. Mars, with its fierce energy, reminded him of the friends who ignited their passions and drove them to be better, always ready to stand by their side in every challenge.

Jupiter, with its expansive wisdom, was like the mentors and teachers in their lives, those who helped expand their minds and dreams. Mercury, quick and adaptable, was like the neighbours and acquaintances whose words and ideas shaped the everyday exchanges of life, always bringing fresh perspectives and new ways of thinking.

Venus, the planet of love and beauty, symbolized the daughters, sons, and loved ones who brought grace, harmony, and deep emotional connection into their lives. The Moon, with its reflective light, was like the friends who understood their innermost feelings, those who mirrored their souls and shared their deepest secrets.

And finally, the Sun—his father believed it to be the core of the family, the source of life and warmth, much like the parents who guided them, provided for them, and lit the path ahead.

As the son reflected on these comparisons, he saw the truth in his father's words. The people in their lives were like planets in a cosmic dance, each playing a vital role, each influencing the course of their journey. This dance of relationships was where the true beauty of life was found—where each step, each interaction, created the rhythm of their existence.

Son, I've seen families build and fade,
In time's embrace, their stories laid.
Some bonds are forged in such a way,
That when one leaves, the other strays.

In love, they lived so intertwined,
Two souls, one heart, one single mind.
Their days were shared, their nights the same,
A tender dance, a cherished flame.

But life is cruel, and time unkind,
It takes away, leaves grief behind.
And when one passes from this life,
The other faces endless strife.

For how can one, so deeply bound,
Find strength to stand on hollow ground?
When half their soul has flown away,
How can they greet another day?

I've seen them linger, shadows faint,
Their spirits worn, their hearts a plaint.
For in their love, they were so near,
That life without seems too severe.

So close they lived, so close they loved,
That when death came, it barely shoved.
The other, left in silent grief,
Barely clings to life, a fragile leaf.

Yet in their sorrow, there is grace,
A testament to love's embrace.
For even when they're torn apart,
They carry half the other's heart.

Reflection 10: A Love So Close

As we journey through life, we often witness the incredible power of love in its most profound form. There's a particular kind of love that transcends the ordinary, binding two souls so closely together that they become almost inseparable. It's a love that doesn't just fill their days with joy but also intertwines their very essence, so much so that when one departs from this world, the other is left grappling with a void that seems impossible to fill.

This kind of love is both a gift and a burden. It brings immense happiness and fulfilment, yet it also carries with it the potential for deep sorrow. When we love so deeply, we risk experiencing the profound pain of loss. But even in that pain, there is a beauty—a testament to the strength of the bond that was shared.

The poem *A Love So Close* speaks to this duality of love. It captures the delicate balance between the joy of connection and the grief that follows when that connection is severed by death. The poem reflects on the enduring impact of such a love, showing how the surviving partner, though burdened by loss, continues to carry a part of their loved one within them. This is the weight of deep love—it lingers long after the person is gone, shaping the lives of those left behind.

In these moments of sorrow, there is also a sense of grace. The love that once brought two people together continues to live on, not just in memories but in the way it influences every thought, decision, and action. It's a reminder that while love can bring us to our knees in grief, it also lifts us, guiding us through life, even after those we love have passed on. This reflection reminds us that such love, though heavy, is a precious legacy, one that continues to shape our hearts and lives long after the physical presence is gone.

The Legacy of Places - 11

Yesterday, we walked this path so bright,
With laughter and stories, our hearts took flight.
Where sunlight danced through leaves up high,
And the earth held our footprints, warm as July.

Together, we carved moments in the air,
Etched in time, memories beyond compare.
Friends and family, hand in hand,
Every step a treasure, every glance a strand.

But today, as I wander this trail alone,
The trees still stand, but the warmth has flown.
Everything feels foreign, shadows take hold,
As if the world shifted, leaving stories untold.

The places we cherished now whisper so low,
With echoes of laughter, where no smiles grow.
No touch, just silence, a strange empty space,
Where memories linger, yet time leaves no trace.

Nothing was stored, nothing remains,
The echoes of our days now hold only pains.
I walk past these moments, recalling the days,
That once made this place feel like home in so many ways.

Reflection 11: The Legacy of Places

As the son's journey through his father's life and legacy came to a close, he found himself reflecting on the physical places that had been part of their lives. These were not just locations or buildings; they were spaces filled with memories, echoes of the past that lingered long after the people had moved on. His father had often spoken about the importance of these places, how they held the essence of their shared experiences, and how they were the repositories of their history.

The son remembered the paths they had walked together, the rooms where they had spent countless hours talking, laughing, and sometimes just sitting in comfortable silence. These places had been witnesses to their lives, holding within them the joy, sorrow, love, and loss that had shaped their family. His father had taught him that these places, though often taken for granted, were sacred in their own way. They were the anchors that connected them to their past and provided a sense of continuity as they moved forward.

But as the son revisited these places in his mind, he realized that they were no longer the same. Time had changed them, and without the people who had once filled them with life, they felt different—empty, almost unfamiliar. Yet, even in their changed state, these places still held the memories, the invisible threads that tied him to his father, to his family, to the life they had shared.

The son understood that while these places might change, the memories they held would remain a part of him forever. They were the silent keepers of his father's legacy, the physical manifestations of the love and life that had been so precious. As he prepared to carry on with his own life, he knew that these places and the memories they held would always be with him, guiding him, comforting him, and reminding him of where he came from.

Tears of the Heart - 12

In the quiet moments of the day,
When words are few and light gives way,
A simple gesture, soft and kind,
Can leave an imprint on the mind.

A hand that reaches, not for show,
But out of love, pure and slow,
A smile that warms like morning sun,
In these small acts, love has begun.

Respect is woven, thread by thread,
In silent words that go unsaid,
And in these threads, a heart is caught,
By all the care that can't be bought.

The tears that come, not out of pain,
But from a joy that can't be feigned,
For in the smallest things, we see,
The love that sets our spirits free.

Reflection 12: Tears of the Heart

As the son reached the final stages of his journey through his father's legacy, he began to understand that the most powerful emotions often emerged in the quietest moments. His father had always been a man of few words, preferring actions over grand expressions, but those actions had left a lasting imprint on the son's heart. It was in the small, seemingly insignificant gestures that the depth of his father's love and care truly revealed itself.

The son remembered how his father would offer a comforting hand during tough times, a reassuring smile when words failed, and a quiet presence that made everything feel just a little bit easier. These moments weren't about grand displays of affection; they were about the unspoken understanding, the silent support that said more than words ever could. His father had taught him that love didn't always need to be loud or visible—it could be as gentle as a breeze, as steady as a heartbeat, and still be profoundly felt.

As he looked back on these moments, the son realised that these small acts of love had been the foundation of their relationship. They were the threads that had woven them together, that had created a bond that would last beyond this life. And in remembering these moments, the son felt a sense of peace and gratitude, knowing that his father's love would always be with him, in every gesture, in every smile, in every quiet moment of reflection.

These memories, though often accompanied by tears, were not tears of sorrow, but of joy and remembrance. They were a testament to the life they had shared, the love that had shaped them, and the legacy that would continue to guide him long after his father was gone.

A Time Well Spent - 13

Either with football or with cricket stump,
In every game, my heart would jump,
But when not on the field in flight,
I would sit with parents, teachers in sight.

Childhood days, both wild and free,
As house captain, proud to be,
Representing my school with grace,
Each task embraced, each challenge faced.

Assignments and homework, written with pride,
With teachers and parents close by my side.
The radio hummed with games afar,
We would dream of victory, each like a star.

Matches played on fields of green,
A battle between teams, so keen.
But most of all, the wisdom gained,
From parents and teachers who patiently explained.

Their stories shaped our youthful years,
Guiding us through both joys and fears.
A time when dreams began to soar,
When childhood was so much more.

Reflection 13: A Time Well Spent

Reflecting on those school days, the son realises the profound impact of each experience. Whether it was the thrill of playing football or cricket or the quiet moments spent learning from parents and teachers, every moment was an essential part of his growth.

Serving as house captain, he learned responsibility, teamwork, and leadership. The role taught him to represent his group with pride, face challenges head-on, and embrace each task with dedication. With assignments and homework, teachers and parents were always by his side, encouraging him to balance academics with other pursuits.

Each task and challenge he took on back then seemed small, yet collectively, they shaped who he is today. Those were the days when his dreams began to take flight, rooted in the values and lessons imparted by those who came before him.

Now, as he looks back, he sees that it truly was a time well spent—a foundation for the future laid with joy, guidance, and the unforgettable moments of a childhood filled with purpose.

The Web of Life - 14

In the web of life, connections strong,
We find the place where we belong.
Each thread we weave, each bond we make,
Adds to the strength, the paths we take.

Through friends and family, near and far,
We build a network, like a guiding star.
Each face we meet, each hand we hold,
Becomes a part of the story told.

No one walks this path alone,
In every heart, a seed is sown.
The ties we form, the love we share,
Create a legacy beyond compare.

For in the end, it's not what we own,
But the connections we've made, the love we've shown.
These are the treasures we leave behind,
A lasting bond, forever entwined.

So, cherish each thread in the web we spin,
For it's through these links that our lives begin.
And as we journey, side by side,
It's the strength of these bonds that will guide.

Reflection 14: The Web of Life

As the son neared the end of his journey through the memories and wisdom his father had left behind, he found himself reflecting on the legacy of connection that had been such a central theme in his father's life. His father had always believed that a person's true wealth lay not in material possessions, but in the relationships they built, the bonds they formed, and the connections they maintained with those around them.

His father's life had been a testament to this belief. He had been a man who valued every relationship, whether it was with family, friends, neighbours, or even those he encountered briefly. He saw each person as a thread in the intricate tapestry of life, each connection adding richness and colour to the whole.

The son remembered how his father had always been there for others, offering support, guidance, or simply a listening ear. He understood that these connections were not just a part of his father's life—they were the essence of it. They were what had given his father's life meaning and purpose.

As the son looked at his own life, he realised that these connections had also shaped him. The relationships he had with others, the bonds he had formed, were all influenced by the example his father had set. And now, as he thought about the future, he knew that it was these connections that would carry his father's legacy forward.

His father had taught him that no one is truly alone in this world; we are all connected in ways both visible and invisible. And it is through these connections that we find strength, comfort, and the true meaning of life. The son knew that if he maintained these connections, his father's legacy would continue to live on.

The Strength of the Heart - 15

In the quiet battles fought alone,
Where light is dim, and hope is sown,
A strength emerges, deep and true,
A force that guides, that carries you.

Not in the loud, triumphant roar,
But in the silent, steady core.
The heart that beats through darkest night,
That finds the will to stand and fight.

It's in the calm, the quiet grace,
The way you hold your steady pace.
Through every storm, through every test,
The heart that strives, that never rests.

This strength is more than muscle or might,
It's the inner fire, the guiding light.
The courage to face what lies ahead,
To rise again from where you've bled.

For in the heart, true power lies,
Beyond the reach of worldly ties.
It's the legacy of those who've gone,
The silent strength that carries on.

So, hold it close, this strength within,
Let it guide you to where life begins.
For in the end, it's this, you'll see,
That shapes your path, your destiny.

Reflection 15: The Strength of the Heart

As the son continued to reflect on the wisdom his father had imparted, he found himself contemplating the inner strength that had always guided his father through life's challenges. His father had a quiet resilience, a kind of strength that didn't manifest in grand gestures or loud proclamations but in the steady, unwavering beat of his heart. This strength was rooted in his father's deep sense of purpose, his commitment to his values, and his unshakable belief in the power of perseverance.

The son remembered how his father had faced difficult times with a calm resolve, never allowing the weight of the world to crush his spirit. Whether it was dealing with personal loss, financial hardship, or the everyday struggles that life inevitably brings, his father had always found a way to endure, to keep moving forward. This was not because he was immune to pain or sorrow, but because he had learned to draw strength from within, from the core of his being.

His father had taught him that true strength doesn't come from physical power or external success; it comes from the heart. It's the ability to stand firm in the face of adversity, to hold onto hope when all seems lost, and to keep fighting for what you believe in, even when the odds are stacked against you. This inner strength, his father had said, was the most valuable asset one could possess.

As the son thought about his own life, he realised that this strength of heart was something his father had passed down to him. It was the legacy of resilience, the ability to weather life's storms without losing sight of who you are or what you stand for. And as he moved forward on his own path, he knew that this strength would continue to guide him, just as it had guided his father.

The Rhythm of Life - 16

Life's rhythm flows, a gentle tide,
A dance we learn as time goes by.
It lifts us up, it pulls us down,
In every smile, in every frown.

We rise with hope, we fall with pain,
But in each step, we rise again.
The waves that crash, the winds that blow,
Are part of life's unceasing flow.

It's in the balance we find our grace,
The steady heart, the quiet pace.
In every high, in every low,
We find the strength to let life flow.

The seasons change, the tides will turn,
And through it all, we live and learn.
To dance with life, to feel its beat,
To move in time with every feat.

For in this rhythm, we find our peace,
A gentle calm, a sweet release.
The joy in knowing, come what may,
Life's rhythm guides us on our way.

So, trust the waves, embrace the ride,
Let the rhythm be your guide.
For in this dance, we find our place,
In life's eternal, timeless grace.

Reflection 16: The Rhythm of Life

As the son continued to reflect on his father's teachings, he began to appreciate the natural rhythms that his father had always seemed to understand. His father lived his life in harmony with these rhythms, moving with the ebb and flow of time, seasons, and circumstances. There was a grace to the way his father navigated life, an acceptance of both the joys and the sorrows, the successes and the failures, as part of a greater, natural cycle.

The son recalled how his father often spoke about the importance of recognising these rhythms, of understanding that life is not a constant upward climb but a series of waves—sometimes lifting us high, sometimes pulling us low. His father taught him that it was essential to learn to move with these waves, to find balance and peace in the knowledge that neither the highs nor the lows would last forever. Life, his father had said, was about finding harmony within this rhythm.

This perspective had helped the son through many difficult times. When life seemed overwhelming, his father's words reminded him to breathe, to step back, and to trust in the natural course of things. The rhythm of life was not something to be fought against, but something to be embraced, to be danced with, just as his father had always done.

As the son reflected on his own life, he realized that this understanding of life's rhythm had shaped his approach to challenges and opportunities alike. It had taught him patience, resilience, and the ability to find joy even during struggle. And as he moved forward, he knew that this rhythm would continue to guide him, helping him navigate whatever lay ahead.

The Light of Legacy - 17

A legacy is not just what we leave,
In wealth or words, for those who grieve.
It's in the lives we touch each day,
In every choice, in every way.

It's in the kindness we extend,
To stranger, neighbour, foe, or friend.
It's in the love we give so free,
A lasting mark, a memory.

For when we're gone, what will remain?
Not gold or silver, not wealth or fame.
But the light we cast in life's brief span,
The way we lived, the way we ran.

It's in the hearts we've helped to heal,
The truths we've spoken, bold and real.
It's in the hands we've held with care,
The burdens lightened, the love we share.

So, as you walk your path each day,
Remember what you give away.
For in each act of love or grace,
You leave a light, you leave a trace.

A legacy that shines so bright,
Guiding others through the night.
It's not in stone or in the grave,
But in the lives you've helped to save.

This is the light that will not fade,
The legacy of love you've made.
So live each day with heart and soul,
And let your legacy make others whole.

Reflection 17: The Light of Legacy

As the son neared the end of his reflections on his father's life, he found himself contemplating the concept of legacy. His father had lived a life that was not only rich in experience but also deeply meaningful in the way it touched others. The son understood that legacy wasn't just about what one leaves behind in material terms; it was about the values, the lessons, and the love that continue to influence the lives of those left behind.

His father had often spoken about the importance of living with purpose, of making choices that would leave a positive mark on the world. He had taught the son that legacy was not something you consciously create; it was the natural result of living a life of integrity, compassion, and dedication. It was the light that would continue to shine long after you were gone, illuminating the paths of those who followed.

The son realized that his father's legacy was not just in the words he had spoken or the actions he had taken, but in the way he had made people feel—loved, valued, and supported. It was in the quiet moments of kindness, the steady guidance, and the unwavering commitment to doing what was right. This legacy was now a part of the son's life, guiding him just as it had guided his father before him.

As he reflected on his own life, the son felt a deep sense of responsibility to carry this legacy forward. He knew that he, too, would one day leave behind a light for others to follow. His father had shown him the way, and now it was up to him to continue that journey, to live in a way that honoured the values his father had instilled in him, and to pass those values on to the next generation.

The Circle of Life - 18

Life is a circle, round and wide,
Where every turn begins inside.
From birth to death, and back again,
The circle spins, without an end.

Each joy we feel, each tear we cry,
A part of life's eternal sky.
For every end brings something new,
A chance to start, a chance to view.

The lessons learned, the paths we tread,
Are never lost, they're never dead.
They come around in different ways,
In different times, on different days.

For life's a dance, a winding road,
With each new step, a fresh new code.
We move in rhythm, side by side,
In the circle where all things abide.

So when you face an end in sight,
Remember there's another light.
For in the circle, life renews,
With every dawn, with every bruise.

We find our way, we find our peace,
In the circle, that will never cease.
For every turn, we learn to grow,
In the endless dance, the endless flow.

And as we walk this path so true,
We leave behind the old for new.
In the circle, we find our place,
A legacy of love and grace.

Reflection 18: The Circle of Life

As the son contemplated the final lessons his father had imparted, he found himself reflecting on the cyclical nature of life. His father had always viewed life as a continuous journey, one where beginnings and endings were intertwined, where every end was simply the start of something new. This perspective had given his father a deep sense of peace, allowing him to face life's challenges and changes with grace and acceptance.

The son remembered how his father had spoken about the importance of understanding this cycle. He had taught the son that life was not linear but circular, with every experience leading back to another, creating a rich tapestry of interconnected moments. His father believed that every joy, every sorrow, every success, and every failure was a necessary part of this cycle, contributing to the growth and evolution of the soul.

This understanding had helped the son navigate his own life, especially during times of transition and loss. His father's wisdom had shown him that life's challenges were not obstacles but opportunities for renewal, for beginning again with a deeper understanding and a stronger heart. It was a lesson that had given the son strength and resilience, helping him to see the beauty in both the highs and lows of life.

As the son looked forward to the future, he knew that this cycle would continue and that the lessons his father had taught him would one day be passed on to others. The circle of life, as his father had described it, was endless, always evolving, always returning to where it began. And in this circle, the son found comfort, knowing that his father's legacy would continue to live on, not just in his memories but in the lives of those who came after him.

Embracing Change – 19

Life's River flows, it never stays
In one still place, in one set phase.
It winds and turns, it ebbs and flows,
Taking us where the future grows.

Change is the current, strong and wide,
It pulls us along; it shapes our ride.
We can't resist, we can't remain,
For life is movement, joy and pain.

In every twist, in every turn,
There's something new for us to learn.
A lesson found, a strength revealed,
In every change, a wound is healed.

For in the flow, we find our way,
Through dark of night, to light of day.
We learn to bend, we learn to grow,
To let the changing waters flow.

So, when the river takes you far,
To lands unknown, to distant star,
Remember this, you're not alone,
For change is where new life is sown.

Embrace the shift, embrace the tide,
Let it take you where dreams reside.
For in the end, it's change that shows,
The path of life, where love still grows.

Reflection 19: The Gift of Change

As the son neared the conclusion of his reflections, he found himself contemplating the inevitability of change. His father had always approached change not with fear but with an open heart and a willingness to adapt. He understood that change was an essential part of life's journey—a force that shapes us, challenges us, and ultimately helps us grow.

The son recalled how his father faced various changes throughout his life—changes in circumstances, relationships, and the relentless passage of time. His father had taught him that change was not something to resist; rather, it was something to embrace. It was through change that they uncovered new opportunities, discovered hidden strengths, and learned invaluable lessons.

His father often likened life to a river, continuously flowing and moving forward. To resist change was akin to trying to hold back the river—a futile endeavour. Instead, he encouraged his son to move with the current, to allow the flow of life to carry him to new places, experiences, and understandings. This perspective instilled in the son the courage to face the unknown and step into the future with confidence and hope.

Reflecting on his own life, the son recognised that the changes he had experienced, though sometimes challenging, contributed to the person he had become. Each change marked a step on his journey, an integral part of his growth into who he was. As he looked ahead, he understood that change would remain a constant companion, guiding him toward new horizons and shaping his path in ways yet to be revealed.

The Echoes of Wisdom - 20

In quiet halls where shadows play,
The echoes of wisdom find their way.
They linger soft in every breath,
A guiding light that conquers death.

They whisper truths in silent hours,
In every thought, their subtle powers.
They shape our lives, they guide our hand,
A legacy so softly planned.

For wisdom isn't loud or grand,
It's in the things we understand.
It's in the moments when we pause,
To see the world, to find the cause.

These echoes come when least we seek,
In moments strong, in moments weak.
They're there to guide, to help us see,
The paths that lead to destiny.

They carry on from sire to son,
From daughter's hand to everyone.
They're in the choices that we make,
The silent vows we never break.

For wisdom lives in every heart,
A timeless gift, a priceless art.
It echoes on, from past to now,
A silent force that shows us how.

So, listen close, when silence falls,
To the wisdom echoing in these halls.
It's in the love, the lessons learned,
In every truth our hearts have earned.

Reflection 20: The Echoes of Wisdom

As the son delved deeper into the memories of his father, he began to realise that his father's wisdom was not just a collection of lessons or advice but a living, breathing presence that echoed through every aspect of his life. These echoes of wisdom had shaped his decisions, guided his actions, and provided comfort during times of uncertainty. His father's voice, though now silent, continued to resonate in the son's heart and mind, offering guidance long after he was gone.

The son recalled countless moments where his father's words had come back to him, sometimes in the most unexpected ways. Whether it was a piece of advice that suddenly made sense in a new context or a simple phrase that had grown in meaning over the years, his father's wisdom had a way of reappearing just when it was needed most. These echoes were more than memories; they were the living legacy of a man who had devoted his life to teaching, guiding, and loving those around him.

As the son reflected on his own life, he realised that these echoes of wisdom had become a part of him, inseparable from his own thoughts and beliefs. They were the foundation upon which he had built his life, the steady hand that had guided him through both joy and sorrow. And as he looked toward the future, he knew that his father's wisdom would continue to echo through the generations, shaping not only his life but the lives of those who came after him.

The son understood now that his father's legacy was not just in the lessons he had taught but in the way, those lessons continued to live on, evolving and growing as they were passed down from one generation to the next. These echoes of wisdom were timeless, a bridge between the past and the future, connecting the son to his father in a way that would never fade.

The Power of Silence - 21

In the quiet hush of evening light,
Where words are few and thoughts take flight,
There lies a power, soft and true,
In the silence shared between us two.

No need for words, no need for sound,
For in this stillness, love is found.
A quiet bond, a steady grace,
Reflected in each other's face.

Silence speaks in ways so deep,
In the promises that we keep.
It tells of strength, it tells of care,
A silent vow that's always there.

In the pauses, in the space,
We find a gentle, quiet place.
Where hearts connect without a word,
And every thought is softly heard.

For silence holds a world inside,
A place where tender truths reside.
It's where we go when words are weak,
To find the answers that we seek.

So, when the noise of life is loud,
And voices rise, and thoughts are proud,
Remember this, the silent way,
Where wisdom has the final say.

In the silence, we find what's real,
The truths that words can't quite reveal.
It's in this quiet, still embrace,
That we discover love's true face.

Reflection 21: The Power of Silence

As the son reflected on the many lessons life had imparted, he found himself thinking about one of the most profound aspects of his father's character—his ability to convey so much through silence. His father had always been a person of few words, preferring to let his actions speak for him. Yet, it was in the moments of silence that the son often felt closest to understanding his father, sensing the depth of his thoughts and the strength of his convictions.

He remembered the countless times they had sat in silence, whether during a quiet evening at home, a long walk in the countryside, or even in the midst of a family gathering. These moments were never awkward or uncomfortable; they were filled with a quiet understanding and mutual respect that didn't need to be spoken aloud. His father's silence was not an absence of communication but a different kind of dialogue, one that spoke directly to the heart.

Through these experiences, the son learned that silence could be powerful, that it could convey things that words often fail to express. Silence could be a source of comfort, a way to show support without intrusion, and a space where true understanding could flourish. It was in these silent moments that he often found clarity, and a sense of peace that helped him navigate the complexities of life.

As he looked back on his journey, the son realised that this ability to embrace silence was one of his greatest strengths. It was a reminder that not everything needed to be said and that sometimes, the most profound connections were those that were felt rather than spoken. And as he moved forward, he carried with him the power of silence, knowing that it would continue to guide him just as his quiet moments always had.

A shame it was, to lose the rank,
Not to be in cricket, nor the army's flank.
The barest pass, just scraping by,
Yet never enough to truly fly.

A haunting shadow, this life of mine,
A career that meets the barest line.
To aim, to race with the competent few,
But the struggle is fierce, the wins are few.

How hard it is, this race I run,
When others start where I'm nearly done.
To reach the base—my only aim,
While others rise to heights of fame.

Is it the need to simply belong,
That keeps me fighting, keeps me strong?
To stand at the base and watch them soar,
While I'm content to strive for more.

And when they asked, "What's your next quest?"
I smiled and spoke of Everest.
Then paused, and softly I confessed,
"The base camp, at least, to start the rest."

For the base is where my journey starts,
A place to soothe my weary heart.
Not the summit, but a place to dream,
Where future heights may yet be seen.

Reflection 22: The Struggle to Belong

The son often reflected on the struggles that had shaped his life, particularly the battle to find a place where he truly belonged. He understood these struggles not with bitterness but with a quiet resignation and understanding. Life, he realised, was not always about reaching the highest peaks but sometimes about simply finding a place to stand, a baseline from which to build.

He remembered the disappointments of not achieving certain goals, whether in sports or career advancements. These moments left deep scars, times when he felt he had failed to meet the expectations placed upon him by society, by his peers, and most painfully, by himself. But instead of giving up, he continued to push forward, determined to at least reach the baseline, the place where he could begin again.

This struggle to belong and to be recognised was a recurring theme in his life. The need to prove oneself, to show that one was worthy of being included, was a powerful force, one that drove him to keep fighting even when the odds were stacked against him.

Yet, through all the struggles, there was also a sense of acceptance. He came to realise that his worth was not determined by reaching the top but by the effort he put into the climb. For him, reaching the baseline was an achievement in itself, a place where he could pause, regroup, and dream of future heights. This resilience, this ability to find strength in simply belonging, even if it meant standing at the base and watching others soar, became a guiding principle.

His journey was a reminder that everyone's path is different. Some are meant to reach the summit, while others find their peace at the base. The important thing, he understood, was to keep striving, to keep dreaming, and to find contentment in knowing that he gave it his all, even if the summit remained out of reach.

The Power of Faith in Uncertainty -23

Son, where faith resides and plans are laid,
The journey begins, though shadows shade.
The road ahead seems hard, unclear,
No path in sight, no way to steer.

Yet trust in faith, let it guide,
A path will build as you stride.
Step by step, with courage in hand,
The road will rise, like shifting sand.

Invisible now, but soon to unfold,
A journey long, with tales untold.
The destination, though far from sight,
Will come to pass, in the warmth of light.

Reflection 23: The Power of Faith in Uncertainty

Son, there are moments in life when the road ahead seems uncertain, where the path appears blocked, and no clear way forward is visible. It is in these moments that faith becomes our compass. Faith, combined with thoughtful planning, has the power to shape our journey, even when the destination seems distant and the obstacles insurmountable.

As you walk through life, remember that the road may not always be visible. It may seem that there is no way forward, but as you take each step, the path will begin to build itself beneath your feet. It may be challenging, and the journey may test your resolve, but with faith as your guide, the road will extend, carrying you toward your destination.

Faith is not merely a belief in the unseen; it is the force that creates the way forward. When plans are aligned with faith, the impossible becomes possible, and the journey, though long and arduous, will lead to the place you are meant to be. Trust in the process, have faith in your steps and know that the road will appear, even when you cannot yet see it.

The Journey of an Idea – 24

From heaven's heights where spirits dwell,
A seed of thought begins to swell.
It journeys down on wings of light,
To find a mind in darkest night.

A spark of hope, a dream so pure,
Drifts through the streets with no detour.
It seeks a heart that hears the call,
To catch the whisper, rise, and sprawl

In fleeting moments, many sense,
The brush of brilliance, so intense.
Yet fears, distractions, doubts untold,
Let slip the gift, so bright, so bold.

But one lone soul, with pen in hand,
Embraces what the winds command.
A story forms, a world renewed,
In her, the vision's seed is strewed.

From thought to word, to action swift,
The world now feels the quiet shift.
An idea's path from mind to pen,
Transforms the earth, again, again.

So in this town where dreams align,
Let whispers find a soul divine.
For those who heed the heaven-sent plea,
Shape tomorrow's destiny.

Reflection 24: The Journey of an Idea

From the highest reaches of heaven, where the seeds of creation are born, a singular idea began its journey toward Earth. It carried within it the potential to bring about profound change—a pure and radiant thought, waiting to be nurtured and manifested in the physical world.

As the idea descended, it sought a mind that could recognise its divine origin, a vessel through which it could take form. It moved with purpose, yet with patience, scanning the hearts and minds below. It touched many briefly, testing their readiness, but found that distractions, fears, and doubts clouded their receptivity.

Undeterred, the idea continued its search, moving through the ether with a quiet determination. It knew that somewhere, someone would be attuned to the subtle vibrations of its presence, prepared to grasp the depth of its meaning and the significance of its potential.

When at last the idea found a mind open enough to receive it, it did not hesitate. It entered gently, like a breath of wind, infusing thoughts with clarity and purpose. In this moment of connection, the idea began to unfold, its essence flowing naturally into the mind that was ready to embrace it.

Here, in this sacred space of thought, the idea found life. It was no longer just a whisper from the heavens but was becoming a tangible reality, shaped and guided by the mind that had welcomed it. The transformation had begun.

And so, the idea continued its journey, moving from the realm of thought into the world of action. It would not rest until it had fulfilled its purpose, bringing about the change it was meant to inspire.

In the silence that followed, other ideas began their descent, each searching for a mind ready to receive them, to nurture them, and to bring them into the world, just as this one had done.

No Privacy, No Secrets - 25

In a world where shadows speak
And privacy is but a weak,
Fleeting dream, a passing thought,
Secrets play, their lessons taught.

What's withheld is power stored,
A hidden strength, a silent sword.
For when the time is ripe and right,
It strikes, unseen, within the night.

They play their games with subtle hands,
Holding cards like shifting sands.
What's unknown is soon erased,
But what is shared is never placed.

So, son, be wise, keep things inside,
Let silence be your trusted guide.
For what is hidden stays at bay,
But what's revealed may haunt someday.

Reflection 25: No Privacy, No Secrets

The son often found himself pondering the complexities of privacy in a world where shadows speak, and secrets lurk. He understood that in the absence of discretion, what was once sacred often became exposed, leading to questions about the strength of what remains hidden. Secrets, he realised, hold a hidden power, a silent strength that can emerge at the right moment, much like a blade drawn in the dark.

In this landscape of shifting sands, he reflected on the subtle games played by those around him, where what is known is easily erased, yet what is shared carries weight. He wondered about the balance between openness and discretion, knowing that letting too much slip can leave one vulnerable to regret. The wisdom of silence became clear to him—a trusted guide in a world eager for revelation.

He questioned the moments when he had chosen to share, the times he had opened up, and what those revelations had cost him. As he looked around, he sought to understand how much of himself he should keep inside and how much was safe to reveal. What was hidden could stay at bay, but what was unveiled might linger and haunt him in ways he couldn't foresee.

In the quiet corners of his mind, the son recognised the importance of safeguarding his inner world. He understood that true power lies not in the act of sharing everything but in discerning what should remain private. This journey of understanding the value of secrets and silence would ultimately shape the legacy he hoped to impart to his children—a lesson about the strength found in discretion and the importance of knowing when to keep things close to the heart.

The Crumbing Home – 26

Once, there were homes, warm and bright,
With festivals blooming in radiant light.
Families gathered, songs filled the air,
Dancing and laughing, without care.

Jokes and joy, hearts intertwined,
Moments of love, so sweetly aligned.
The walls stood strong, the days so grand,
We held it all in the palm of our hand.

But now I see the homes fade away,
The walls crumble, memories stray.
The voices drift in whispers low,
Of times long gone, where did they go?

The bodies leave, the spirits roam,
What was once ours is no longer home.
A strange voice calls from depths unknown,
Reminding us how much has flown.

For all we had, is none today,
The homes grow quiet, the light gives way.
Yet in my heart, the echoes stay,
Of laughter, love, and yesterday.

Reflection 26: The Crumbing Home

As the son stood at the threshold of his old family home, he couldn't help but reflect on how much had changed over the years. The once-vibrant house, filled with the sounds of festivals, laughter, and togetherness, now felt like a shell of its former self. The walls, which once echoed with songs and joy, seemed to hold only silence now. The gatherings that used to fill the home with warmth and love had become distant memories, and the spirit of the place seemed to have drifted away with those who had left.

He remembered how they used to celebrate every occasion with full hearts, surrounded by family and friends. The air would be thick with love, the scents of food, and the sounds of shared laughter. Those days felt indestructible, as though nothing could ever change the bond that held them together. Yet, now, the son stood alone, feeling the absence of the life that had once thrived within these walls.

As time passed, the world had shifted. People had moved on, seeking new paths, and the home that once united them had crumbled, not just physically but emotionally. The spirit that had made it a home was gone, replaced by a quiet that felt almost foreign.

Still, despite the emptiness, the son held onto the echoes of what once was. The memories of laughter and love lived on in his heart, and he found comfort in knowing that those moments, though lost to time, had shaped him into who he was. The crumbling home was a reminder of the inevitable passage of time, but it was also a reminder of the strength of the bonds that transcended it.

Echoes of the Unseen - 27

Where did I falter, and what slipped from my grasp?
In the depths of my heart, I ponder and clasp.
Tracing back to the skills that I sought,
The education that shaped me, the lessons I've taught.

The confidence that fuelled me, the spirit that soared,
With dreams set on peaks, I bravely explored.
But what did I truly create on this quest?
What walls did I breach, what trials put to test?

What steps did I skip, and what treasures forgot?
In lands that whispered tales, I pondered a lot.
I pause to reflect on the truths that I've found,
What wisdom did I grasp as I travelled around?

What lessons did the journey kindly bestow?
As I gaze at the faces, their stories in tow.
I'm left to wonder what moments I missed,
What dreams did I forfeit, what chances dismissed?

With my children near, their futures so bright,
I'm left to reflect on the legacy's light.
What gifts did I share, what love did I weave?
In echoes of unseen, I hope they believe.

Reflection 27: Echoes of the Unseen

The son often found himself in quiet moments of introspection, questioning the choices he had made and the paths he had taken. He would trace his steps back to the days of learning and growth, recalling the skills he had once sought, the education that had laid his foundation, and the knowledge that had sharpened his understanding of the world. These were the building blocks of his life, the elements that had shaped his craft fuelled his confidence and lifted his spirit on wings of hope.

But despite all that he had gained, there lingered an unshakable sense of uncertainty. What had he truly created with all that he had acquired? What walls had he breached in his quest for achievement? There were moments he couldn't help but wonder about the steps he might have missed, the opportunities that might have slipped through his grasp, and the treasures that lay forgotten along the way.

His dreams had always been set on the highest peaks, driven by a determination to carve out a place for himself in the world. He had journeyed through lands rich with ancient tales, leaving his mark in places that echoed with history and meaning. But as he paused to reflect, he couldn't help but ask himself—what truths had he unveiled? What wisdom had he truly grasped? And what lessons had his journey offered?

In the faces of those he encountered, in the smiles of those he passed by, he sought answers to these lingering questions. He wondered about the moments he might have overlooked, the dreams he might have surrendered in the pursuit of his goals. And as he looked into the eyes of his children, their futures bright and full of promise, the questions deepened.

What legacy had he truly bestowed upon them? What gifts had they embraced, and what had they left behind?

The son knew that his journey was far from over. The echoes of the unseen—those moments of missed opportunity, the silent lessons, and the unspoken truths—continued to resonate within him. They were the questions that would guide him forward, shaping the legacy he hoped to leave behind.

The Burden of Fulfillment - 28

He met each duty with steady hand,
Yet in his heart, a question stands:
Did he pause to weigh the right,
Or simply follow duty's light?

When hopes dissolved, and dreams unmade,
The family's anger sharp as blade,
Struck him down, with no forewarning,
Echoes of a silent mourning.

Old wounds, now fresh, from shadows came,
Accusing eyes, his heart to blame,
He wondered where he lost his way,
Did all his efforts go astray?

He gave, he cared, he did his best,
But doubts now stirred within his chest,
Was it feeling that misled his stride,
Or the lack of cold reason's guide?

In this storm of unspoken grief,
He sought the truth, yet found belief,
That obligation, though sincere,
Can't always calm the hidden fear.

He'll carry on, but with a tear,
For what was lost, for what's unclear,
And in the silence of the night,
He'll search for peace within the fight.

Reflection 28: The Burden of Fulfillment

The son often found himself questioning the true nature of his responsibilities and the burdens that came with fulfilling them. Throughout his life, he had approached each duty with a steady hand, doing what was expected of him without hesitation. But in the quiet moments, when the weight of the day's obligations gave way to introspection, he couldn't help but wonder if he had truly weighed the right course of action or if he had simply followed the path laid out by duty.

As the years passed, he encountered moments where hopes dissolved and dreams were left unfulfilled. These moments often brought with them a sharp sense of disappointment, not just from within but from those around him. The family's expectations, once a source of motivation, sometimes became a heavy burden, striking him down with the force of unspoken anger and silent mourning. Old wounds, once thought healed, would resurface, accompanied by accusing eyes that seemed to question his very worth.

In these difficult times, the son would ask himself where he had gone astray. Despite giving his best, despite caring deeply, doubts would stir within him, casting shadows over his efforts. Was it his emotions that had misled him? Or had he failed to apply the cold, rational reasoning that might have steered him in the right direction?

Caught in a storm of unspoken grief and inner turmoil, the son sought the truth. He came to understand that even sincere obligation could not always calm the fears that lurked beneath the surface. There was a profound realisation that fulfilling duties, no matter how well-intentioned, could sometimes lead to unintended consequences and leave behind a trail of unresolved questions.

Yet, despite the pain and uncertainty, he knew he had to carry on. The burden of fulfilment was not something he could simply set aside. He would continue to meet his responsibilities but with a tear for what was lost and for what remained unclear. And in the stillness of the night, he would search for peace within the ongoing fight, hoping to reconcile his sense of duty with the need for inner peace.

The Call of the Mountain - 29

Today, I visited the mountain's face,
Though rarely I go, I find my place.
The sun dips low, the shadows long,
The path awaits, a silent song.

It was hard at first, a painful climb,
For a man untrained, unversed in time.
The steep ascent, the fading light,
The rocks and trees, bathed in twilight.

But day by day, I climbed anew,
The path, once feared, no longer grew.
No longer hard, no longer strange,
The mountain's call, a steady change.

The path now waits, it knows me well,
Each twist and turn, each rise and fell.
I've found my places where I rest,
Before I push on with the quest.

Reaching the top, with sunset's glow,
The descent is quick, the world below.
Yet still, I rise to climb each day,
Though why I do, I cannot say.

For as the sun begins to fade,
My heart remembers, unafraid.
The mountain may forget my tread,
But I recall each step I've led.

The mountain calls, I hear it clear,
A silent voice I hold so dear.
In its embrace, I find my way,
A guide through night, to greet the day.

Reflection 29: The Call of the Mountain

The son had developed a ritual, a pilgrimage that brought him to the face of the mountain whenever he felt the need to reconnect with his thoughts and emotions. The mountain had become more than just a physical challenge; it was a sanctuary, a place where he could find clarity amidst the chaos of life.

In the beginning, the climb had been difficult, a painful struggle for a man untrained and unversed in the demands of such a journey. The steep ascent and fading light seemed to conspire against him, and the rocks and trees, bathed in twilight, appeared as obstacles rather than companions. But he persisted, returning to the mountain whenever the urge struck him, slowly acclimating to its rhythm.

As time passed, the path that once filled him with trepidation began to feel less daunting. The mountain's call, which had once been a challenge, now became a steady and reassuring presence in his life. The path no longer felt hard or strange; it was a journey he knew well, with its twists and turns, its rises and falls. He had found his places of rest along the way, where he could pause and gather his strength before pressing on.

Reaching the top, as the sun cast its final glow over the landscape, had become a moment of quiet triumph. The descent, swift and sure, brought him back to the world below, yet still, he felt the pull to return to the mountain whenever his spirit needed it. There was something inexplicable in this routine, a deep need to climb, even when the reasons weren't entirely clear to him.

The mountain, in its silent majesty, had become a part of him. It may forget the tread of his footsteps, but he would never forget the journey it had led him on. Each step he took up its slopes was a step toward understanding himself, toward confronting the challenges within. The mountain's call was more than a beckoning of the earth; it was a call of the soul, one that he held dear and answered whenever the moment was right.

The Vanishing Flame - 30

The power in the halls, once bold,
Exhausts like fire, growing cold.
In no time, it flickers, fades,
As people pass through shifting shades.

Hands that grasped with greedy might,
Now vanish in the endless night.
The chair they held, the words they spoke,
Drift away like rising smoke.

For when the flame of power dies,
And silence takes its place, it lies—
That person, once revered, admired,
Is forgotten, their name expired.

Others have passed, claimed their space,
Grabbing power, quick to erase
The one who held it not long before,
Now, just a shadow, nothing more.

The world moves fast, it doesn't stay,
For power's fleeting, like the day.
And those who seek to hold it tight,
Soon find themselves lost in the night.

So let your strength be more than fame,
Not bound to power's fickle flame.
For in the end, it's love, not might,
That holds us in the lasting light.

Reflection 30: The Vanishing Flame

In *The Vanishing Flame*, the son contemplates his father's thoughts on power and legacy. His father had witnessed, time and again, how those who sought power often found themselves consumed by it, only to be forgotten once their influence faded. The son now realises that his father never placed much value on power for power's sake; instead, he believed that true strength came from within, from love, integrity, and the bonds we build with others.

The poem speaks to the fleeting nature of power, likening it to a flame that will eventually fade no matter how brightly it burns. The son remembers how his father would often remind him that while power might bring temporary respect or admiration, it is not what endures. Instead, it is the quiet acts of kindness; the love shared, and the legacy of goodness that lives on long after the flame of power has died out.

As the son reflects on this, he understands the deeper wisdom his father tried to impart: that real strength is not in how much control or authority one can wield but in how much love and light one can spread. His father's life was a testament to this belief. Though he may not have sought fame or recognition, his influence was far-reaching, grounded in the love and respect he earned from those around him.

The son now carries this lesson forward, knowing that while power fades, the love and compassion we show others will remain, lighting the way long after the flame of influence has vanished.

Relatives, my son, are the ones who remain,
Rare in their qualities, enduring the strain.
They share in our moments, both joy and strife,
Settling the scores that linger in life.

But in each exchange, seek a clear way,
To leave no dents that time might delay.
Speak with them openly, don't wait for the clock,
Resolve what you can, be the steady rock.

As you walk past, keep your heart clean,
Not just for you, but for all who have been.
Make no grand promises, don't over-extend,
For relatives are many; know where they stand, my friend.

Let your bond be simple, yet sincere,
With respect for their place, and for all they hold dear.

Reflection 31: The Mirror of Relatives

Relatives are the ones who remain in our lives through all seasons, sharing in our joys and sorrows. Their presence can be a source of support but also a mirror reflecting the complexities of family dynamics. In your interactions with them, seek clarity and resolution. Address issues openly and honestly, and avoid making promises you cannot keep. Keep your relationships simple yet sincere, respecting the bonds that have been formed over time. By doing so, you maintain a sense of harmony and respect within the family, ensuring that these ties remain strong and true.

Son, understand the ones who took your aid,
May not remember, may not parade.
Given the chance, they may not engage,
But those who helped you, keep the balance stage.

Relatives are great to share in delight,
Invite them to occasions, keep things light.
But distance, my son, is wisdom's embrace,
Keep them close, yet know their place.

Reflection 32: The Balance of Relatives

Relatives play a significant role in our lives, but it is important to understand the balance in these relationships. Some may forget the help you've offered, while others may not engage as you hoped. It is essential to recognise who truly supports you and to keep the balance in your interactions. Invite relatives to share in joyous occasions, but also maintain a healthy distance. Knowing their place in your life helps you navigate these relationships with wisdom, ensuring that your connections remain positive and fulfilling.

The Path to Wisdom - 33

Son, tread your path with careful grace,
Each stage you meet has its own place.
To skip a step is to lose your way,
For wisdom's roots in stages stay.

Jumping ahead may seem so swift,
But shortcuts often lead to rifts.
Many have tried to leap the line,
Only to find their steps misaligned.

Experience is the guide you need,
Though old wisdom can plant the seed.
Learn through each stage, let each one teach,
For skipping steps may leave you out of reach.

The paths are laid for those who dare
To walk them fully, step by step, with care.
Don't discount the journey's slow advance,
For each stage holds its own special chance.

Embrace the time, let wisdom grow,
In every phase, let lessons show.
The journey's worth is in the climb,
In every stage, you'll find your time.

Reflection 33: The Path to Wisdom

As the son continued to navigate the challenges of his life, he often found himself reflecting on the wisdom his father had shared with him over the years. One piece of advice that echoed in his mind was the importance of experiencing each stage of life fully, without rushing or attempting to bypass the lessons each phase had to offer.

His father had often spoken about the dangers of shortcuts, reminding him that while it might be tempting to leap ahead, true wisdom was rooted in the gradual accumulation of experience. Skipping steps, his father had warned, could lead to misalignment and missed opportunities for growth. The son realised that this advice was not just about the practicalities of life but about understanding the deeper truths that each stage of life had to teach.

He remembered his father's words: "Experience is the guide you need, though old wisdom can plant the seed." This advice had guided him through many difficult moments, reminding him to take his time, to let each phase of life unfold naturally. It was through this careful progression that he had learned to appreciate the journey itself, understanding that wisdom was not something to be rushed but something to be cultivated with patience and care.

As he reflected on his own path, the son knew that his father's teachings had shaped his approach to life. He had come to see that each stage held its own unique opportunities for learning and growth and that the journey was just as important as the destination. The wisdom his father had imparted was a gift that continued to guide him, helping him to navigate the complexities of life with grace and understanding.

The Power of Belief - 34

People fight for reasons deep,
Their struggles, dreams, and secrets keep.
Each battle fought, a testament true,
To the beliefs that guide them through.

These fights are more than simple strife,
They shape their path, define their life.
In every clash, a feedback received,
A way to grow, to be relieved.

Their self-belief, a force so strong,
Empowers them to right the wrong.
Respect themselves, they come to know,
A combination that helps them grow.

So as they strive, let them be,
Their journey's marked by bravery.
Hurt not their spirit, nor their quest,
For in their fight, they seek their best.

Honour their path, their strength, their will,
For these are what their hearts fulfil.
In every struggle, there's a spark,
Guiding them through shadows dark.

Reflection 34: The Power of Belief

As the son reflects on "The Power of Belief," he is reminded of the countless struggles his father faced with unwavering determination. His father's life was not one of ease but one defined by battles—both internal and external—fuelled by a deep sense of belief in himself and in the values that guided him. The son now sees that these struggles were not merely hardships but vital moments of growth and self-realisation.

His father had always taught him that the true measure of a person was found in their ability to stand firm in their beliefs, even when the world around them seemed unsteady. Every challenge was an opportunity to refine oneself, strengthen resolve, and build character. The poem captures this idea perfectly: that belief is not just a passive feeling but a driving force that shapes one's destiny.

The son now understands that his father's quiet strength came from this deep-seated self-belief, a belief that allowed him to move through life's trials with grace and resilience. His father had always respected the struggles of others, knowing that each person's journey was marked by the battles they fought within themselves. The son recognizes that it was his father's belief in both himself and in others that created an enduring legacy of strength and compassion.

Through his father's example, the son has learned that belief is the light that guides one through life's darkest moments, and it is in honouring that belief—in oneself and in others—that true growth and fulfilment are found.

Son, see how the rich have shaped their kin,
With ease and wealth, they're born to win.
Their children inherit fruits so sweet,
Yet miss the lessons, the path's heartbeat.

Kings make kings, the wealthy do the same,
Their legacy is set in gold and fame.
But true growth lies not in ease bestowed,
But in the garden each of us must grow.

The poor teach their children of meagre days,
Of hard work's struggle, of life's rough ways.
In every lesson, in every strife,
They impart the skills to thrive in life.

We all aim to give our children more,
Yet the richest gift is wisdom's core.
For it's not in riches, nor in crowns of gold,
But in the effort and the stories told.

Teach them to sow, to tend, to reap,
To understand the seasons deep.
In each stage of life, let them find their way,
For true growth comes from the journey, day by day.

Reflection 35: The Garden of Growth

The son often pondered the differences between those who were born into wealth and those who had to carve their path through hard work and perseverance. His father had frequently spoken of this, drawing a clear distinction between the ease that wealth could provide and the true growth that came from facing life's challenges head-on.

He had observed how the wealthy often passed down their fortunes to their children, setting them on a path of ease and comfort. But his father had warned that while these children might inherit riches, they often missed out on the deeper lessons of life—the lessons that could only be learned through personal effort and struggle. "Kings make kings, the wealthy do the same," his father would say, "but true growth lies not in ease bestowed, but in the garden each of us must grow."

His father's words had instilled in him a profound understanding of the value of hard work and the importance of guiding children through their own experiences. It wasn't enough to simply give; the true gift was in teaching them to find their way, to sow their own seeds, and to tend to their own gardens. It was in these efforts and in the stories that were shared along the way that real wisdom was passed down.

The son knew that while it was natural to want to give his children more than he had, the richest gift he could offer them was the wisdom to navigate life's challenges on their own. It was about teaching them the skills to thrive, not just to survive, and to understand the seasons of life deeply. For true growth, his father had taught him, came not from what was inherited but from the journey of learning and growing each day.

The True Path to Wisdom - 36

The old taught us how to face defeat,
In failure's art, their lessons meet.
They showed the price of **greed, of strife,**
The heavy toll of an ambitious life.

Yet wisdom's thread was oft unspun,
For it's not just in battles won.
It's not in hoping for things to change,
Or waiting idly for fate to arrange.

True wisdom lies in walking time's road,
With purpose firm and a steady load.
It's in embracing each trial's test,
And learning from the struggle's quest.

It's not in dreams or passive ease,
But in the striving that brings peace.
To grasp the depth of wisdom's way,
One must engage in each day's play.

So, tread with confidence, embrace the fall,
For in each step, is wisdom's call.
It's forged in effort, not in luck,
In the journey's grit and the spirit's pluck.

Reflection 36: The True Path to Wisdom

As the son reflected on the teachings of his elders, he recognised the depth of the lessons they had imparted, particularly in how to face defeat and navigate the complexities of life. The older generation had taught him the art of failure—not just how to endure it, but how to learn from it, how to grow stronger through the setbacks that life inevitably brings. They had shown him the heavy toll of unchecked ambition and greed and the pitfalls that lay in wait for those who pursued life's battles without wisdom.

But as he delved deeper into these teachings, the son realised that wisdom was not solely found in avoiding mistakes or overcoming failures. True wisdom, as he came to understand, was not about passively hoping for change or waiting for fate to take its course. It was about actively engaging with life, walking time's road with purpose and resolve, and embracing each trial as an opportunity to learn and grow.

His father had often spoken of the importance of striving, of putting in the effort, even when the outcome was uncertain. It was through this active engagement with life, through the daily grind and the challenges faced head-on, that true peace and understanding could be found. Wisdom was not something that came easily or by chance; it was forged in the fires of experience through the grit of the journey and the courage to face each day's trials.

The son knew that to truly grasp the depth of wisdom, he had to be willing to embrace the falls as well as the victories. It was in the journey, in the effort, in the spirit of perseverance that the real lessons were learned. His father's teachings had instilled in him the understanding that wisdom was not a destination but a path—one that required constant engagement, effort, and a willingness to learn from every step along the way.

A Woman's Dilemma - 37

The house, a canvas yet to be,
With dust and clutter plain to see,
She wonders if it's worth the try,
To welcome friends or let it lie.

Each corner holds a task undone,
A chore that waits, a battle won,
Yet still, she hears that quiet voice,
To gather friends—could it be a choice?

The floors might gleam, but not enough,
The shelves arranged, but still too rough,
She ponders if they'll see the flaws,
Or simply come with warm applause.

Her mind it races, heartbeats swift,
To open doors or let them drift,
For hosting's more than just a space,
It's baring all in every place.

She fears the gaze that might critique,
The eyes that judge, the words that speak,
But deep within, she knows it's true,
They come for her, not for the view.
A gentle nudge from love's own hand,
Reminds her of what they'll understand,
That friendships thrive in warmth and grace,
Not in the shine of a spotless place.

So she contemplates, in quiet thought,
The worth of joy that could be sought,
And as the evening stars align,
She finds the courage, pure, divine.

For, in the end, it's love that wins,
The laughter shared, where it begins,
And so she chooses, brave and bright,
To let them in and to the light.

The house, it may not be pristine,
But in its walls, a warmth unseen,
For friends will see beyond the dust,
To what is real, to what they trust.

Reflection 37: A Woman's Dilemma

In "A Woman's Dilemma," the son reflects on a struggle he witnessed not only in his mother but also in his wife—both women, at different times, facing the inner conflict of wanting to present a perfect home while fearing judgment. The poem captures the universal tension between societal expectations of perfection and the deeper understanding that true relationships are built on love, not appearances.

As the son reads the words, he recalls how his mother would often question whether the house was tidy enough, worrying about the opinions of guests. His father would gently remind her that true friends come not to assess the home but to share in the warmth and love it holds. Similarly, he has seen his wife go through the same dilemma, wondering if their home is "presentable" enough for visitors. But in both women, he sees a quiet strength that eventually shines through—a realization that love and connection matter far more than the external trappings of a perfect home.

The son is struck by how his mother and wife have navigated this delicate balance and how his father, with his calm and reassuring words, always knew that true friendships are built not on appearances but on understanding. The poem beautifully captures this truth as the woman comes to realize that her friends care more about the joy and warmth she brings to the gathering than the dust on the shelves.

Through this reflection, the son honours the quiet wisdom of his mother and wife, acknowledging that their journeys mirror one another. Both women, with their grace and strength, have taught him that love and friendship thrive in the authenticity of shared moments, not in the pursuit of perfection. It's a lesson passed down through the generations, rooted in the understanding that the relationships we nurture, not the space we inhabit, truly matter.

The Paradox of Gifted Paths – 38

The rich may gift their children's way,
For they have walked through time's own fray.
They've carved the paths, made trails so clear,
Yet wish their kin would not draw near.

Why give the ease and comforts grand,
If you believe they should not withstand?
Son, this is a paradox so wrong,
For the path of ease can't make them strong.

To shield from struggle is to miss
The lessons wrapped in hardship's kiss.
The journey through the trials and tests,
Is what builds strength, what shapes the best.

Gifts of comfort, wealth, and ease,
Cannot replace the skills to seize.
For wisdom blooms from effort's seed,
Not from avoiding what you need.

So, understand, my child, the lore,
That gifts of ease are not the core.
It's through the struggle and the strife,
That you'll discover the depth of life.

Reflection 38: The Paradox of Gifted Paths

The son often reflected on the paradox he observed in the lives of those born into wealth and privilege. It was a contradiction that his father had pointed out to him many times—the idea that while the rich may gift their children with paths of ease, they also express a desire for their offspring to develop strength, resilience, and wisdom. But how, his father had asked, could these qualities be nurtured in the absence of struggle and challenge?

His father's teachings had made it clear that the paths carved out by wealth and privilege, though well-intentioned, often deprived children of the very experiences that would help them grow into strong, capable individuals. The comforts and ease provided by their parents could not replace the lessons wrapped in the hardships of life. It was through facing trials and overcoming obstacles that true strength was forged.

The son understood that this paradox was a fundamental flaw in the way many viewed success and inheritance. The rich, in their desire to provide for their children, might inadvertently weaken them by shielding them from the struggles that build character and resilience. His father had always emphasised that wisdom and strength were not gifts that could be handed down; they were earned through effort, through the willingness to engage with life's difficulties.

This understanding had shaped the son's own approach to life. He knew that while gifts of comfort and wealth had their place, they could never replace the invaluable lessons learned through personal struggle. The journey through trials and tests was essential, not just for survival, but for truly thriving and discovering the depths of life. His father's words reminded him that it was the effort, the striving, and the courage to face life's challenges that ultimately led to wisdom and fulfillment.

Echoes of Yesterday - 39

I walked that path again,
Through trees and rocks, beneath the rain.
The mountains clouds, all stood in line,
As though they'd never once been mine.

Nothing had changed; the views were still,
The sunset is blocked by the distant hill.
I've seen it all, I know the sight,
But now I'm lost, out of their light.

Once I belonged, now I've moved on,
No longer needed, I am gone.
No witness left, no place to stay,
A part of me has slipped away.

The days have passed, my place erased,
Yesterday, a dream was displaced.
A memory now I can't convey,
No voice to hear, no time to stay.

These moments given, wrapped in care,
Are fleeting now, no longer there.
And though they lived, they drift, they fall,
As if they never lived at all.

Reflection 39: Echoes of Yesterday

"Echoes of Yesterday" explores the feeling of returning to a once-familiar place and realising how time has distanced the speaker from it. Though the physical surroundings remain unchanged, the speaker feels like a stranger, no longer part of the moment or the memories. This evokes a sense of isolation as the past fades and loses its place in the present. The poem reflects on the fleeting nature of memory and how, when left unshared, it can feel as though it never existed at all. Ultimately, it's a meditation on time's quiet ability to erase not only moments but also our connection to them.

The Loss of Legacy - 40

Son, I've read of kings of old,
Whose wealth and power, grandly told,
Were seized by heirs with greedy hands,
Who turned on those with whom they'd stand.

The children sought the riches vast,
Yet didn't grasp the lessons passed.
In their hunger for the prize,
They overlooked the wisdom's ties.

Elders fell to ruthless schemes,
Their hard-won gains now shattered dreams.
The legacy they left behind,
Lost in folly, unrefined.

For wealth and power, without the guide,
Becomes a burden, far and wide.
Without the wisdom to sustain,
The treasures fade, the gains are vain.

So remember, child, as you strive,
It's not just wealth that keeps dreams alive.
But the wisdom to guide what's earned,
And the lessons from the past you've learned.

Reflection 40: The Loss of Legacy

The son often contemplated the tales his father had shared with him about the downfall of great legacies. These stories were not just about the kings and rulers who had amassed wealth and power but also about the tragic loss of what they had worked so hard to build. His father, drawing from the lessons of history, often spoke about how easily these legacies could be squandered when passed into the hands of those who lacked the wisdom to sustain them.

His father had read about kings whose wealth and power were seized by their heirs—children who, in their greed, failed to grasp the deeper lessons their parents had tried to impart. These heirs, eager to claim their inheritance, often turned on those who had once stood by their side, driven by a hunger for riches that blinded them to the true value of the legacy they were meant to uphold.

The son understood that his father was trying to teach him an important lesson: that wealth and power, without the guidance of wisdom, could easily become burdens rather than blessings. The elders in these stories had fallen victim to ruthless schemes, and their hard-won gains were reduced to shattered dreams, lost in the folly of those who came after them.

The legacy left behind, his father emphasised, was not just about the material wealth that was passed down. True legacy lies in the wisdom and values imparted to the next generation. Without this wisdom, the treasures of the past could fade, and the gains could prove to be in vain.

His father's words served as a reminder that as he pursued his own goals and ambitions, it was not just wealth that would keep his dreams alive. It was the wisdom to guide what was earned and the lessons learned from the past that would ensure the preservation and appreciation of any legacy he hoped to leave behind.

The Circle of Opportunity – 41

Son, in time, you'll come to see,
The man your father was, who he came to be.
The world moves in a steady grace,
And what's lost today will return to its place.

When chance is lost, don't be dismayed,
For time's wise circle will have its way.
Prepare yourself, stay sharp and keen,
For when the door reopens, it's then you'll glean.

The world will spin and bring anew,
The chances that once slipped from view.
Be ready for the moment's call,
And seize the chance when it does fall.

For understanding comes with time,
And you will find your steady climb.
Embrace the cycle, and you will find,
The chance that waits, just right behind.

Reflection 41: The Circle of Opportunity

The son often reflected on the opportunities that had come and gone in his life, sometimes with a sense of regret for those he had missed. His father had always reassured him that the world operated in cycles and that what seemed lost could often return in time. This was a lesson his father had imparted with great emphasis, encouraging him to stay prepared and vigilant for the moments when opportunities would reappear.

His father had spoken of the world's circular nature, how time moved in patterns that often brought back the chances that once seemed lost. The key, he had taught his son, was to remain ready—to sharpen his skills, to stay keen and alert— so that when the door of opportunity opened once again, he would be ready to walk through it.

The son learned to embrace this cyclical view of life, understanding that missed chances were not always gone forever. Instead, they were part of a larger rhythm, a dance of time that would eventually bring those chances back around. It was in this understanding that he found a new kind of patience, a readiness to seize the moment when it came, armed with the lessons and preparations he had made during the waiting period.

His father's wisdom became a guiding principle in his life, reminding him that the circle of opportunity was always turning. The moments that slipped away would return, and when they did, he would be ready to grasp them fully. This cyclical nature of opportunity gave him a sense of peace and confidence, knowing that life would offer him multiple chances to achieve his goals as long as he remained prepared.

The Paradox of Wealth – 42

Son, I've seen the wise with wealth so grand,
Who tightly hold their hard-earned hand.
They save their coins with utmost care,
Yet suffer want, a stark affair.

In sickness, they forego the cure,
And hunger finds them insecure.
Their riches, tightly grasped and stored,
Are seldom used, though they afford.

Their clothes are plain, their homes austere,
In contrast with the wealth they steer.
The life they lead, so far removed,
From what their earnings could have proved.

They fear the loss, the spending spree,
Yet live in want, as you can see.
For wisdom, it seems, does not abide,
When hoarding wealth, needs are denied.

So understand, my child, this truth:
True wisdom's not in wealth aloof.
It's in the balance, the use, the care,
To live with purpose, not just spare.

Reflection 42: The Paradox of Wealth

The son often pondered the stories his father shared about those who amassed great wealth yet lived in surprising deprivation. His father, drawing from both observation and historical accounts, often spoke of the irony he had seen among the wise and wealthy—individuals who had carefully saved and accumulated their riches but were reluctant to spend even on their own needs.

His father's tales painted a picture of people who, despite their vast resources, lived lives of unnecessary austerity. They clung tightly to their wealth, fearing loss or waste, and as a result, they often denied themselves the basic comforts that their wealth could easily provide. The son heard stories of those who forewent medical care in times of sickness, skipped meals out of insecurity, and lived in plain homes with modest clothing, all while sitting on fortunes that could have afforded them a much more comfortable life.

The paradox, as his father explained, was that while these individuals were wise enough to amass wealth, they lacked the wisdom to use it meaningfully. Their fear of spending, of losing what they had worked so hard to earn, trapped them in a cycle of want and insecurity despite their riches. His father's lessons underscored that true wisdom wasn't just in the ability to save and accumulate but also in knowing when and how to use wealth to live a purposeful and fulfilling life.

The son understood that his father was teaching him a valuable lesson about balance. Wealth, while important, was not the ultimate measure of success or happiness. It was in the thoughtful and purposeful use of resources that true wisdom was found. The fear of spending, when it led to a life of unnecessary deprivation, was as much a trap as poverty itself. His father's words encouraged him to seek a balance between saving and living, to use wealth wisely, not just to hoard it.

Son, I've seen the lavish play,
Wealth lost in chance, gone in a day.
While those in need, with hopeful hearts,
Dream of wealth torn apart.

The rich may waste what poor ones seek,
In fleeting joy, their riches leak.
The toil of many, lost in jest,
While fortune's wheel spins its quest.

Heed the stars and tales of woe,
What's wasted high is needed low.
For every loss in reckless hands,
Could save a life on poorer lands.

A toss, a spin, a fleeting game,
For some, it's fun, for others, shame.
In every gamble, there's a sign—
The waste of some could save a line.

Reflection 43: The Gamble of Fortune

The son often reflected on the stories his father told him about those who gambled away their fortunes in reckless pursuits. His father had seen and read about many lavish souls who, despite their wealth, risked everything on the whims of chance. These individuals, caught up in the fleeting excitement of gambling, often lost in a single moment what others could only dream of possessing.

His father had pointed out the stark contrast between the lives of these wealthy gamblers and those of the poor who struggled daily to make ends meet. While the rich could afford to waste their wealth on vain amusements, the poor could only watch from the sidelines, their hopes pinned on the possibility of a better life. The money that the wealthy squandered in a single night could have been a lifeline for those in need, a way to lift themselves out of poverty and secure a future for their families.

The son understood that his father was imparting a lesson about the responsibility that came with wealth. The grandeur lost in reckless jest, as his father called it, was not just a personal loss for the gambler but a missed opportunity to make a difference in the lives of others. The poor, who toiled and struggled every day, could only dream of the riches that the wealthy treated so carelessly.

His father's words served as a reminder that wealth should not be taken for granted or wasted on fleeting pleasures. Instead, it should be used with care and consideration, recognising its potential to create positive change. The son learned to see the value in every dollar, understanding that what might seem like a small loss to one person could be a significant gain for another. His father's teachings encouraged him to be mindful of how he used his resources, to avoid the pitfalls of reckless spending, and to always consider the impact of his actions on those less fortunate.

The Wisdom of Wealth - 44

Son, know this truth of wealth's domain,
It is wisdom, not mere toil, that can truly sustain.
Fun and labour, though they may strive,
Cannot grasp the riches where wisdom must thrive.

Wealth dances with cunning grace,
A force that can deceive, then swiftly erase.
It plays with the mind, a game profound,
Where escape or failure can swiftly be found.

In the realm of gold and grand allure,
Only wisdom's touch can ensure it's secure.
For wealth, in its essence, holds a mystic guise,
And only the wise can navigate its complex ties.

So, seek not just the gains of fleeting mirth,
But also the wisdom that anchors true worth.
For in understanding the nature of wealth's art,
You find the strength to hold and never depart.

Reflection 44: The Wisdom of Wealth

The son often contemplated the nature of wealth and the responsibilities that came with it. His father had always emphasised that wealth, while desirable, was not merely a product of hard work or luck. Instead, it required a deep understanding—a wisdom that could guide its accumulation, management, and use. His father's teachings had instilled in him the knowledge that without wisdom, wealth could easily become a fleeting and deceptive force, one that could lead to ruin as quickly as it could bring prosperity.

His father had spoken of wealth as something that danced with a cunning grace, a force that could deceive those who sought it without the proper understanding. He had warned his son that wealth could play with the mind, offering illusions of security and success, only to erase them in an instant if not approached with wisdom. The son had learned that the pursuit of wealth required more than just toil and labour; it required a careful and thoughtful approach, one that recognised the true nature of wealth and its potential to either uplift or destroy.

The son understood that wisdom was the anchor that could secure wealth, allowing it to be managed and used in a way that brought lasting value. His father had taught him that without wisdom, wealth could easily slip through one's fingers, leaving behind only regret and loss. It was this wisdom that allowed the truly successful to navigate the complexities of wealth, ensuring that it served its true purpose rather than becoming a source of endless pursuit and anxiety.

The son knew that his father's words were not just about financial wealth but about the broader understanding of value in life. The wisdom to manage wealth was intertwined with the wisdom to live a balanced and meaningful life, one that did not place material gain above all else. His father's teachings guided him to seek not just the accumulation of wealth but the understanding of its true worth and the wisdom to use it wisely.

The Wisdom of Power – 45

In the realm where power reigns,
Responsibility and wisdom flow in streams,
A force that gives, yet plays with dreams,
Where decisions aren't always as they seem.

Power brings with it a weighty trust,
A mantle of duty, a test of just.
Yet, in its grasp, the mind can sway,
Tempted by desires that lead astray.

Experience whispers truths from time,
Revealing how and when events align.
It stirs within a hunger deep,
A thirst for more that makes us weep.

But wisdom holds the guiding light,
Through the maze of dark and bright.
It tempers greed and guards the soul,
And steers the course to a balanced goal.

Power's allure can cloud the sight,
And only wisdom keeps it right.
In the dance of wealth and might,
It's wisdom alone that shines so bright.

Reflection 45: The Wisdom of Power

The son often reflected on the nature of power and the responsibilities that came with it. His father had spoken at length about the delicate balance required to wield power wisely. Power, as his father had taught him, was not merely a tool for achieving one's desires but a force that carried immense responsibility and demanded a careful and thoughtful approach.

His father had described power as something that could easily sway the mind, tempting those who held it to pursue desires that might lead them astray. The son learned that power brought with it a weighty trust—a mantle of duty that tested a person's character and sense of justice. It was a force that could uplift and create but also destroy if not handled with care and wisdom.

Experience, his father had said, was the key to understanding power. Through the lessons of time and the unfolding of events, one could learn when and how to act, recognising the moments when power should be exercised and when it should be restrained. Yet, even with experience, the hunger for more—the thirst for control and influence—could easily cloud judgment, leading to decisions that might later be regretted.

The son came to understand that wisdom was the guiding light needed to navigate the complexities of power. It was wisdom that tempered greed, guarded the soul, and ensured that power was used for the greater good rather than personal gain. His father's teachings emphasised that power, without the balance of wisdom, could become a dangerous force, leading to outcomes that were neither just nor beneficial.

As the son considered his own path, he realised that the pursuit of power, like the pursuit of wealth, required more than ambition. It required a deep understanding of its potential consequences and the wisdom to use it responsibly. His father's words echoed in his mind, reminding him that in the dance of wealth and might, it was wisdom alone that could keep power in check and ensure that it was wielded in a way that honoured both duty and justice.

The Burden of Power - 46

Son, power wields a force that dims,
The spark of youth, the light within.
When one in the family claims its might,
It casts a shadow, hides the light.

In hands that grasp, it subtly spreads,
Affecting all, from parents to beds.
Power, once in grasp, seeps through,
Corroding bonds, as it often will do.

It holds strong, demanding more,
And in its grip, you'll find the core
Of wisdom needed to restrain,
To keep your heart from yielding pain.

For power's lure can overwhelm,
Turning dreams into a broken realm.
Let wisdom guide your careful hand,
To balance what you've come to command.

What is not controlled may soon consume,
And leave you trapped in a darkened room.
So hold with strength, yet wisely tread,
For power's weight can dull the head.

Reflection 46: The Burden of Power

The son had often heard his father speak of power, not as a mere tool, but as a force that carried with it significant burdens. His father had warned him that power, while seemingly desirable, could dim the spark of youth and overshadow the light within if not handled with care. This was a lesson his father had learned from observing how power, once claimed by a family member, could cast a long shadow over everyone around them.

His father had described power as something that, once grasped, subtly spread its influence, affecting not just the one who held it, but everyone in their orbit. It could seep into relationships, corroding the bonds of family and friendship, creating divisions where there had once been unity. The son understood that power, if not checked, could become a demanding force, constantly seeking more and more, and in the process, it could corrode the very foundations of what made life meaningful.

The son learned that the true challenge of power was not in acquiring it, but in managing it wisely. His father had taught him that wisdom was essential to restrain power's potential to cause harm, to ensure that it did not lead to pain and destruction. Power's allure was strong, but without the guidance of wisdom, it could quickly turn dreams into broken remnants of what they once were.

His father's teachings emphasized that power must be held with strength but also with a careful hand. What was not controlled could soon consume the one who wielded it, trapping them in a darkened room of their own making. The son came to realise that power, while necessary at times, was a burden that required balance, caution, and an unwavering commitment to using it justly and wisely.

As the son reflected on his own life, he knew that his father's words were a constant reminder of the importance of maintaining control over power, of not letting it dull his mind or heart. The burden of power was real, but with wisdom, it could be managed, ensuring that it served its true purpose rather than becoming a destructive force.

Power and wealth line the path you tread,
Scattered treasures where your footsteps spread.
Collect them as you journey, handle with care,
Learn their secrets, for they're everywhere.

As you traverse, experience and knowledge blend,
Wisdom emerges, a faithful friend.
It steps in as you grasp to understand,
Guiding you with a steady hand.

In the dance with power and wealth's embrace,
Wisdom becomes your guiding grace.
With its essence clear, you navigate the course,
Harnessing strength from a balanced source.

Only then will you truly see,
The power and wealth in their right decree.
Controlled by wisdom, they'll guide your way,
Illuminating your path **each and every day.**

Reflection 47: The Path of Power and Wealth

The son had often contemplated the intertwined paths of power and wealth, both of which seemed to line the journey of life with their scattered treasures. His father had always advised him to approach these forces with caution and wisdom, understanding that while they could bring great benefits, they also carried significant responsibilities.

His father's teachings emphasised that power and wealth were not simply to be collected as one moved through life. Instead, they were to be handled with care, their secrets learned, and their potential understood. The son had learned that as he traversed the path of life, it was the blend of experience and knowledge that would allow him to grasp the true nature of power and wealth. This understanding would lead to the emergence of wisdom—a faithful friend and guide that would help him navigate the complexities of these forces.

The son understood that in the dance with power and wealth, wisdom was the guiding grace that ensured he stayed on course. His father had taught him that only by embracing the essence of wisdom could one truly harness the strength and potential of power and wealth. With wisdom as his guide, the son knew that he could control these forces, using them to illuminate his path rather than allowing them to lead him astray.

As the son reflected on his journey, he realised that power and wealth, when controlled by wisdom, could guide him in the right direction. They were not ends in themselves but tools to be used wisely and justly. His father's words served as a reminder that the true value of power and wealth lay not in their accumulation but in the way they were balanced and applied in life. With wisdom at the helm, the son knew he could walk the path of power and wealth with confidence and clarity.

The Many Faces of Love - 48

Son, love travels with you, in forms diverse and grand,
Sometimes cloaked in wealth, or power's fleeting hand.
It may disguise itself in wisdom's gentle guise,
Yet, beneath the surface, its true nature lies.

Be cautious with love, for it wears many masks,
Its beauty and mischief are in the tasks it asks.
It dances with allure, both tender and sly,
A friend to beauty and mischief, it cannot lie.

So tread carefully with love, and keep your heart wise,
For its many faces can deceive the eyes.
Embrace its essence, but be mindful of its game,
In its presence, both beauty and mischief claim.

Reflection 48: The Many Faces of Love

The son had often pondered the nature of love, a force that seemed to weave itself through every aspect of life. His father had spoken to him about love's many faces, cautioning that while love was a beautiful and essential part of life, it was also complex and multifaceted. Love could take on different forms, sometimes disguising itself in wealth, power, or even the wisdom that guided one's path.

His father's teachings had emphasised that love was not always what it appeared to be. It could wear many masks, presenting itself in ways that were both alluring and deceptive. The son learned that love could be a friend to both beauty and mischief, capable of bringing great joy but also capable of leading one astray if not approached with care and wisdom.

The son understood that love, while a powerful force for good, required a cautious approach. His father had advised him to tread carefully with love, keeping his heart wise and his mind clear. The many faces of love could deceive the eyes, making it easy to fall for its allure without recognising the potential pitfalls that lay beneath the surface.

As the son reflected on his own experiences with love, he realised that his father's words had been a guiding light. Love, in all its forms, was something to be embraced, but it also needed to be understood and respected. By recognising love's complexity and being mindful of its potential to both uplift and mislead, the son could navigate its many faces with wisdom and grace.

The Pebbles of Emotion - 49

Son, affection, sacrifice, and every tender feeling,
Are like pebbles scattered in the ocean, revealing.
They travel towards you, in waves they come,
To be collected and cherished, each one.

Handle them with care, for they are fragile and dear,
Each emotion a gem, precious and clear.
As they journey to you, in the vast sea's embrace,
Keep them safe, protect their grace.

For in the tides of life, these pebbles hold truth,
The essence of heartache and the warmth of youth.
Guard them closely, with gentle hands,
For they shape the course of your life's sands.

Reflection 49: The Pebbles of Emotion

The son often reflected on the many emotions that had shaped his life, each one contributing to the person he had become. His father had always encouraged him to treat these emotions with the utmost care, likening them to pebbles scattered in the vast ocean of life. These emotions—affection, sacrifice, tenderness—were not just fleeting feelings but precious gems that needed to be collected, cherished, and protected.

His father had taught him that emotions were fragile and easily lost if not handled with care. Like pebbles carried by the waves, they travelled toward him, each one holding a unique significance. The son learned that it was his responsibility to safeguard these emotions, to recognize their value, and to ensure they were not swept away by the tides of life.

As he navigated the complexities of relationships and personal experiences, the son understood that these emotions were the essence of what it meant to live fully. They were the truths that anchored him in times of heartache and the warmth that accompanied the joys of youth. His father's words had instilled in him a deep respect for the power of emotion, teaching him to guard them closely and handle them with gentle hands.

The son came to realise that these emotional pebbles shaped the course of his life's journey. Each one, no matter how small, contributed to the shifting sands of his existence, influencing the direction of his path. His father's wisdom had provided him with the tools to navigate this emotional landscape, ensuring that he remained grounded and true to himself as he collected and cherished the pebbles of emotion that life sent his way.

The Fleeting Nature of Beauty – 50

Son, beauty graces the world for just a fleeting span,
Whether in a lady's charm, a blooming flower's plan,
The rhythm of the tide, or the sunset's golden hues,
It seeks to capture moments and leave its mark on you.

Relish each instance as it unfolds, with wonder and delight,
But be mindful, for beauty's glow fades swiftly from our sight.
It dances briefly in the canvas of time's embrace,
A transient treasure that leaves a delicate trace.

So cherish the moments, for they quickly pass away,
In the fleeting **splendour and wonder** of the day.
Appreciate the beauty while it lasts, with heart and eyes aware,
For it slips through time's fingers, like a breath of air.

Reflection 50: The Fleeting Nature of Beauty

The son had always been captivated by the beauty that surrounded him—whether in the charm of a person, the delicate petals of a flower, or the vibrant hues of a sunset. His father had taught him to appreciate these moments of beauty but also to understand their transient nature. Beauty, as his father often reminded him, graced the world for only a fleeting span, leaving behind a delicate trace as it slipped away.

His father had encouraged him to relish each instance of beauty as it unfolded, to approach it with wonder and delight but also with an awareness that it would soon fade. The son learned to see beauty as a transient treasure, something that danced briefly on the canvas of time before fading into memory. This understanding gave him a deeper appreciation for the moments of splendour that life offered, knowing that they were precious precisely because they were temporary.

The son came to realise that the fleeting nature of beauty was not something to lament but rather something to cherish. It was this very impermanence that made beauty so special, a reminder to live fully in the present and to savour the moments that passed all too quickly. His father's wisdom had taught him to appreciate beauty while it lasted, to be mindful and aware, and to carry the memory of those moments with him as a source of inspiration and joy.

As he reflected on his father's teachings, the son understood that beauty, though brief, had the power to leave a lasting impact. It was a force that enriched his life, even as it slipped through time's fingers like a breath of air. His father's words encouraged him to embrace the fleeting nature of beauty, to see it not as something to hold onto but as something to experience fully and then let go, knowing that its essence would remain with him forever.

The Ephemeral Nature of Fame - 51

Fame, much like beauty, is a fleeting spark,
It shines brightly today but fades with the dark.
It graces you for a moment, a fleeting, dazzling light,
Then slips away, lost to the night.

Today it crowns you with glory and acclaim,
Yet tomorrow, it may be just a name.
It comes with the task, then drifts like the breeze,
Leaving behind only memories and ease.

Cherish the recognition while it's in your sight,
But remember, it's transient, a momentary delight.
For fame, like beauty, is ephemeral and bright,
Gone as swiftly as it came, lost to time's flight.

Reflection 51: The Ephemeral Nature of Fame

The son often thought about the allure of fame and the way it could elevate a person to great heights, only to let them fall back into obscurity just as quickly. His father had always cautioned him about the fleeting nature of fame, comparing it to beauty—a dazzling light that shines brightly for a moment but inevitably fades away.

His father had explained that fame, like beauty, was something to be experienced and appreciated but never to be relied upon. It was a transient spark that could bring glory and recognition today but might be forgotten tomorrow. The son learned that while fame could crown someone with acclaim, it was ultimately a fleeting honour, one that drifted away like the breeze once the moment had passed.

The son came to understand that fame was something to be cherished while it was within reach, but also something to be viewed with a sense of detachment. His father's wisdom had taught him that fame was not a lasting achievement but rather a momentary delight, one that could disappear as quickly as it came. This understanding helped the son stay grounded, reminding him that true worth was not found in the temporary spotlight of fame but in the lasting impact of one's actions and character.

As he reflected on his father's teachings, the son realised that the pursuit of fame, while alluring, was ultimately ephemeral. It was not the end goal but a fleeting experience, one that should be embraced with humility and awareness of its impermanence. His father's words encouraged him to focus on the deeper, more enduring aspects of life rather than becoming consumed by the pursuit of fleeting recognition.

The Journey and the Pebbles - 52

Son, as you gather pebbles and cherish the past,
And hold tight to memories, be sure to travel fast.
While many you encounter may choose to rest,
Remember, your journey is not yet blessed.

Their paths may have ended, their travels complete,
But yours continues with each step you meet.
Do not linger too long where others have stopped,
For your journey unfolds with each new drop.

Collect the moments, but keep moving on,
For the path is long, and much is yet to be won.
The journey awaits with its own unique grace,
So continue forward, and find your own place.

Reflection 52: The Journey and the Pebbles

The son had always been one to gather memories and cherish the moments that shaped his life. His father had often reminded him of the importance of these memories, likening them to pebbles collected along the journey of life. However, his father had also warned him not to let these cherished moments hold him back from continuing his journey.

His father's wisdom emphasised that while it was natural to treasure the past, it was equally important to keep moving forward. The son learned that his journey was not yet complete, and that each new step brought with it the potential for growth and discovery. He was reminded that while others might choose to rest or stop along the way, his own path was still unfolding, and there was much more to explore and achieve.

The son understood that lingering too long in one place, even if it was filled with fond memories, could prevent him from experiencing the full extent of his journey. His father's teachings encouraged him to collect the moments, to value the memories, but also to continue moving forward with purpose and determination. The journey, his father had said, was long and filled with unique opportunities, each one offering a chance to find his own place in the world.

As the son reflected on his father's words, he realised that life was a balance between honouring the past and embracing the future. The journey was ongoing, and while it was important to carry the pebbles of memory with him, it was also essential to keep walking and to continue seeking out new experiences and opportunities. His father's wisdom guided him to appreciate the journey in its entirety, understanding that every step, every moment, was a part of the larger path that would eventually lead him to his true destination.

The Pace of Your Journey – 53

Son, as you walk along your chosen way,
Be mindful of those who rest or stray.
Some rush to compete in a frantic race,
While you move steadily at your own pace.

Their haste may blur their path ahead,
But you tread calmly, where wisdom is led.
In the race of life, they may seek to surpass,
While you find your rhythm, steadfast and steadfast.

So walk your path with quiet grace,
For it is not the speed, but the journey you embrace.
Be aware of the rush, but keep your own tack,
For your journey's value lies in its own unique track.

Reflection 53: The Pace of Your Journey

The son had often observed how others around him seemed to be in a constant rush, competing to reach their goals as quickly as possible. His father had always counselled him to be mindful of this tendency, reminding him that everyone's journey was different and that speed was not always the best measure of success. His father's wisdom encouraged him to walk his path with quiet grace, focusing on his own pace rather than getting caught up in the frantic race of life.

His father had taught him that while others might rush ahead, driven by a desire to surpass their peers, it was more important to find a rhythm that suited his own journey. The son learned that moving steadily and mindfully allowed him to appreciate the experiences and lessons that life offered without being distracted by the haste of those around him. This approach helped him to stay true to himself, following a path led by wisdom rather than the pressure to compete.

The son understood that in the race of life, it was easy to become caught up in the need to keep up with others, to measure success by how quickly one could achieve their goals. However, his father's teachings had instilled in him the value of embracing his own pace, recognising that the journey itself held more significance than the speed at which it was travelled. By focusing on his own path, he could find contentment and fulfilment in the unique experiences that unfolded along the way.

As he reflected on his father's words, the son realised that life's journey was not about rushing to the finish line but about finding meaning and purpose in each step. The pace of his journey was something to be embraced, a reflection of his own values and priorities. His father's wisdom guided him to walk his path with quiet determination, knowing that the true value of his journey lay in the experiences and growth that came with each step, not in how quickly he arrived at his destination.

Guarding Your Journey - 54

Son, as you journey and tread your way,
Beware of those who pause and sway.
They may seek what you've amassed,
Taking from your bounty, moving fast.

Guard well the treasures you collect,
For those who stop may not reflect.
And be wary of the steadfast kind,
Who, with resolve, may seek to find

The fruits of your labour, the gems you've found,
In their pursuit, they may come around.
So keep your heart and hands secure,
For those who linger might not be pure.

In the dance of paths both wide and narrow,
Protect what's yours, let none feel sorrow.
For on your journey, let your wisdom guide,
And shield your treasures with each stride.

Reflection 54: Guarding Your Journey

The son had often been reminded by his father of the importance of protecting the treasures and accomplishments he had gathered along his life's journey. His father warned him that not everyone he encountered would have his best interests at heart. Some might pause on their own paths, eyeing what others had amassed, and seek to take advantage of their hard-earned gains.

His father had emphasised the need to be vigilant, to guard well the fruits of his labour. The son learned that while it was important to share and to help others, it was equally crucial to be cautious of those who might approach with ulterior motives. His father's teachings made it clear that in the dance of life, there were those who might come around, not to contribute but to take from the bounty that had been carefully cultivated.

The son understood that protecting his journey was not just about safeguarding material possessions but also about maintaining the integrity of his heart and mind. His father had advised him to keep his heart and hands secure, to be wary of those who lingered with intentions that might not be pure. The wisdom imparted by his father encouraged him to navigate his journey with both generosity and caution, ensuring that his efforts were not easily undone by others.

As the son reflected on his father's words, he realized that the journey of life was filled with both opportunities and challenges. The key was to remain mindful, to protect what was valuable, and to continue moving forward with confidence and care. His father's teachings provided a guiding light, reminding him that while it was important to embrace the journey, it was equally important to guard it against those who might seek to disrupt or detract from its progress.

The Flow of Time - 55

In time, you'll find, with humour's grace,
That plans and paths may shift their pace.
You set the course, predict the end,
But life, it seems, will always bend.

What you expect is seldom true,
For what unfolds is something new.
Not what you think, but what's revealed,
Is where the truth is truly sealed.

Frustration stems from those who try,
To shape the world beneath the sky.
Halfway through, they grasp for might,
Yet lose the thread, forget the light.

So watch the flow, let it unfold,
Release control, be calm, be bold.
For in the dance of life's design,
It's what occurs that makes it fine.

Reflection 55: The Flow of Time

The future is where your efforts are directed, the horizon you strive toward. Yet, when it's simply handed to you, it loses its meaning, becoming a hollow prize. For those who wish to create and build, the power to shape the future lies in their hands—they can make it as grand or as modest as they choose. But not everyone makes it through. Some are worn down by their struggles, and others lose the will to continue.

The successes that are passed down, seemingly gifts from those who came before, can often be deceptive. They may appear as opportunities, but in reality, they can be tools that shatter your dreams. Beware of receiving things you haven't earned or that come to you before their time. They carry the weight of expectations and the potential to lead you astray.

When you find yourself offered something that feels undeserved or ill-timed, it's crucial to be strong enough to step back. The allure of easy success can be tempting, but it's these very things that can cause the most harm. Only by staying true to your path, and earning each step forward, can you ensure that your future remains yours to create.

The Future's Forge -56

The future's forged by hands that strive,
By dreams and work that keep alive.
But when it's given, without a fight,
It fades away, no longer bright.

Those who craft with heart and soul,
Can shape the world and make it whole.
Yet some are crushed by weight unseen,
And some abandon what might have been.

Success passed down, a fleeting prize,
Can hide the truth beneath disguise.
Beware the gifts that seem so sweet,
They may destroy the dreams you seek.

When offered more than you deserve,
Be cautious, keep your steady nerve.
For easy gains can lead you wrong,
Stay strong, resist, and you'll belong.

Reflection 56: The Future's Forge

The future is shaped by the efforts of those who are willing to work and strive. It is a creation born of dreams and the relentless pursuit of goals.

When success is handed down without struggle, it often loses its value, becoming a hollow achievement. True success is built with intention, resilience, and the will to overcome challenges.

Beware of the allure of easy victories—they may lead you astray. It is in the challenges faced, and the obstacles overcome that the true strength of character is forged. Hold fast to your path and remember that what is earned through effort will always be more rewarding than what is given without struggle.

Mother and Wife - 57

Mother's hand once held you tight,
Guiding you from day to night.
In her care, you grew so wise,
Seeing life through tender eyes.

Then, a wife came to your side,
A partner true, a faithful guide.
She knows your heart, its silent song,
Understands where you belong.

When tears fall or joys arise,
Their love, unspoken, never lies.
In silence or when far away,
They know your soul, come what may.

Take a breath, reflect, be true,
For they can see the real you.

Reflection 57: Mother and Wife

There are two people in your life who know you better than you may know yourself: your mother and your wife.

Your mother nurtured you through the early stages of life, guiding you with wisdom and love. As you grew, your wife stepped in to walk alongside you, sharing in the joys and sorrows of your journey.

Both see the depths of your heart, understanding your unspoken words and silent tears. They are your closest confidantes, knowing you in ways no one else can. Honour the unique bond you share with them, for they see the real you, supporting and loving you unconditionally.

Son, on your journey, you'll meet some who trade,
Offering deals for what you've made.
Be cautious with the bargains they propose,
For their intentions may not always disclose.

A tempting offer might seem fair and right,
But weigh it carefully, with all your might.
In any exchange, you might find,
That starting anew is what's left behind.

So, as you traverse your winding way,
Choose your trades with wisdom's sway.
Each decision, if not made wise,
May lead you to restart and compromise.

Reflection 58: The Caution of Trade

The son had often encountered opportunities to trade or exchange along his journey. His father had always advised him to approach these situations with caution and discernment. While the allure of a tempting deal might seem fair and right in the moment, his father's wisdom had taught him to weigh each offer carefully, considering not just the immediate gains but also the long-term consequences.

His father had explained that in the world of trade, not all intentions were transparent. Some offers might appear beneficial on the surface, but hidden within them could be the potential for loss or compromise. The son learned that it was easy to be swayed by the promise of something new or better, but without careful consideration, these trades could lead to the need to start again, leaving behind what had been painstakingly built.

The son understood that making decisions in the realm of trade required wisdom and a clear understanding of his own values and goals. His father's teachings had instilled in him the importance of choosing trades that aligned with his true purpose, rather than those that might offer short-term benefits at the cost of long-term stability. He was reminded that each decision, if not made wisely, could lead to compromises that would require him to retrace his steps and begin again.

As he reflected on his father's words, the son realised that life's journey was filled with opportunities for trade and exchange, each one offering a chance to grow or to falter. The key was to approach these opportunities with a discerning mind, ensuring that each trade was made with care and intention. His father's wisdom guided him to navigate these decisions with caution, knowing that the choices he made would shape the course of his journey.

The Dream of More - 59

Son, whether you dream of more pebbles to find,
Or a better path that's yet to unwind,
Remember, you need not seek them all,
For what you've earned is a treasure, standing tall.

The journey you've walked, with its trials and gains,
Has given you all that remains.
So cherish the path that you've made your own,
And value the pebbles and lessons you've known.

The dreams of more or a different course,
Are but distractions from your own force.
For you have within all you need to thrive,
In the path you've forged and the life you drive.

Reflection 59: The Dream of More

The son had often found himself dreaming of more—more achievements, more experiences, more paths to explore. His father had always encouraged him to dream but had also imparted the wisdom of appreciating what he had already achieved. His father's guidance emphasised that the journey he had walked, with all its trials and gains, had already provided him with treasures and lessons that were invaluable.

His father had taught him that the pursuit of more was not always necessary. While it was natural to seek growth and improvement, it was equally important to recognize the value of what had already been accomplished. The son learned that the path he had forged, with all its challenges and successes, was a testament to his strength and perseverance. The pebbles he had collected along the way were not just symbols of his journey but also the foundation upon which he could build his future.

The son came to understand that the dream of more, or the desire for a different course, could sometimes be a distraction from the true value of his current path. His father's teachings had instilled in him the importance of finding contentment in the present, of cherishing the lessons and experiences that had shaped him. He realised that within the path he had already walked, he had all the tools and wisdom he needed to continue thriving.

As he reflected on his father's words, the son recognised the power of appreciating the present and the achievements he had already made. The dream of more was not something to

be dismissed, but it was to be balanced with an awareness of
the richness of the life he had already created. His father's
wisdom guided him to see that true fulfilment came not from
endlessly seeking more but from valuing the journey he had
already undertaken.

The Balance of Confidence – 60

Son, be wary of the confidence you build,
For its strength can sometimes be overfilled.
While it can uplift and guide you true,
It may sometimes cast shadows on others too.

Confidence, when strong, can light your way,
Yet its glare can often obscure and sway.
It might dim the light of those around,
Or lead you to a fall from solid ground.

So balance your confidence with care,
Let humility and kindness be your pair.
While confidence can be a guiding star,
It's wise to temper it, lest you stray far.

Reflection 60: The Balance of Confidence

The son had always admired the strength that confidence could bring. His father had often spoken of confidence as a guiding force, something that could light the way and help navigate the challenges of life. However, his father also warned him about the delicate balance needed to wield confidence wisely. Confidence, if left unchecked, could become a double-edged sword—uplifting and guiding on one hand, but potentially casting shadows and causing harm on the other.

His father had taught him that confidence, while essential, needed to be tempered with humility and kindness. The son learned that overconfidence could obscure his judgment, leading him to overlook the needs and feelings of those around him. It could also create a false sense of security, causing him to lose sight of the solid ground on which he stood. His father's wisdom emphasised the importance of being mindful of how confidence influenced not only his own actions but also the dynamics of his relationships.

The son understood that confidence was a powerful tool but one that needed careful handling. His father's teachings had instilled in him the value of balancing confidence with care, ensuring that it did not become overbearing or lead to unintended consequences. By pairing confidence with humility, the son could maintain a clear perspective, allowing him to move forward with assurance without overshadowing others or risking a fall.

As he reflected on his father's words, the son recognised that true confidence was not about always being right or leading the way. It was about understanding when to step back, when to listen, and when to let others shine. His father's wisdom guided him to use confidence as a guiding star, but always

with an awareness of its potential impact. By finding the
right balance, the son could harness the strength of
confidence while remaining grounded, compassionate and
wise.

The Fickle Nature of Support - 61

Son, people around you can bring joy and cheer,
Supporting and guiding, they make things clear.
They're like a match, vibrant and bright,
Cheering you on through the day and the night.

But remember, as the game draws to a close,
Their presence may wane, and away they'll go.
Their support can be fleeting, like a cheer that fades,
Leaving you to navigate the path that remains.

So value their encouragement while it's near,
But be prepared for when they disappear.
For in the end, it's your own strength and might,
That will carry you forward through the darkest of night.

Reflection 61: The Fickle Nature of Support

The son had always appreciated the encouragement and support he received from those around him. His father had often spoken of the joy that came from having others cheer you on, offering guidance and helping to clarify the path ahead. However, his father also reminded him that the nature of support could be fickle—vibrant and strong in one moment but fading away as circumstances changed.

His father had likened support to a match that burns brightly, illuminating the way forward. But just as a match's flame eventually flickers out, so too could the support of others wane when the excitement of the moment passed. The son learned that while it was important to value the encouragement and assistance of those around him, he also needed to be prepared for the times when he would have to rely solely on his own strength and determination.

The son understood that the presence of others could be comforting and motivating, but it was his own resilience that would carry him through the challenges of life. His father's teachings had instilled in him the importance of being self-reliant, of building an inner strength that would sustain him even when external support was no longer available. The son realised that while the cheers and guidance of others were valuable, they were not always permanent, and it was up to him to navigate the path ahead.

As he reflected on his father's words, the son recognised the need to balance appreciation for external support with the cultivation of his own inner resources. His father's wisdom guided him to value the encouragement of others while also being prepared to stand alone when necessary. In the end, it was his own strength and might that would carry him forward, through the brightest days and the darkest nights.

The Caution of Obstacles - 62

Son, on your journey, some may seek to delay,
Their intentions unclear, their path led astray.
They may dwell in their tents, offering a guise,
Promising shelter, yet shrouded in lies.

Be cautious and wise as you move ahead,
For not all who offer will keep you well-fed.
The path may be murky, the road hard to see,
But trust in your heart, let your spirit be free.

Navigate with care, and stay true to your quest,
For obstacles may arise, putting you to the test.
Keep your eyes open, and your purpose in sight,
And proceed with caution through the dark and the light.

Reflection 62: The Caution of Obstacles

The son had encountered various challenges on his journey, some of which came disguised as offers of help or guidance.

His father had often warned him to be cautious of such obstacles, advising that not everyone who appeared to offer assistance had his best interests at heart. His father's wisdom emphasised the importance of being discerning, recognising that some might seek to delay or mislead him, whether out of malice or their own misguided paths.

His father had likened these obstacles to travellers who set up tents along the road, offering shelter but sometimes hiding their true intentions behind a façade of kindness. The son learned that while it was natural to seek refuge and comfort during difficult times, it was also essential to be wary of those who might take advantage of his trust. The path ahead could be murky, with the road hard to see, but his father's guidance had instilled in him the confidence to trust his own instincts and keep his spirit free.

The son understood that obstacles were a part of the journey, often arising when least expected. His father's teachings encouraged him to navigate these challenges with care, staying true to his quest and maintaining a clear focus on his ultimate goals. The obstacles he faced might put him to the test, but with his purpose in sight and his heart guiding him, he knew he could overcome them.

As he reflected on his father's words, the son realised that the journey required both vigilance and determination. While the road might be fraught with difficulties and deceptive offers, he was prepared to face them with wisdom and resolve. His father's teachings had provided him with the tools to proceed with caution, ensuring that he could navigate both the dark and the light with a steady hand and a clear mind.

Passing Down Wisdom - 63

Son, as you tread your path and grow wise,
Share your knowledge as time flies.
When your children start their own life's quest,
Pass on the wisdom you've amassed and blessed.

Though the world may shift and change its face,
The core of wisdom remains in its place.
Generations may come and go,
Yet the truths you've learned will continue to show.

So pass it along with a caring hand,
For the lessons you've gathered will always stand.
In every era, the essence stays true,
Guiding your children as it guided you.

Reflection 63: Passing Down Wisdom

The son had grown wise through the years, his journey marked by countless lessons and experiences that had shaped him into the person he had become. His father had always emphasised the importance of wisdom, not just in acquiring it but in passing it down to future generations. Now, as the son reflected on his own path, he understood the responsibility that came with this knowledge—to share it with his children as they embarked on their own quests.

His father had taught him that while the world might change, the core truths of wisdom remained constant. The lessons learned through trials, successes, and even failures were timeless, serving as a guiding light for those who would follow. The son realised that the wisdom he had gathered was not just for him to hold on to but to pass along with a caring hand, ensuring that his children would be equipped to navigate the challenges and opportunities that lay ahead.

The son understood that wisdom was a precious gift, one that could transcend generations. His father's teachings had provided him with the foundation to build a life of purpose and integrity, and now it was his turn to ensure that these same values were instilled in his own children. By passing down the wisdom he had amassed, he could help them find their way, just as his father had helped him.

As he reflected on his father's words, the son recognised that the act of passing down wisdom was not just a duty but a privilege. It was an opportunity to contribute to the legacy of his family, to ensure that the knowledge and lessons of the past continued to guide and inspire future generations. His father's teachings had taught him that while each generation faced its own challenges, the essence of wisdom remained true, providing the guidance needed to navigate the ever-changing world.

A Shared Journey - 64

Son, as you travel on your way,
You'll find some who struggle and cannot stay.
Lend a hand, and walk by their side,
For their journey, too, is one of pride.

Understand the difference in their stride,
For wisdom guides you from deep inside.
Between two groups, you'll learn to see,
The shared paths and the destinies.

Help them forward, with compassion and grace,
For in their journey, you may find your place.
Let wisdom lead, and you'll discover,
The strength in walking with one another.

Reflection 64: A Shared Journey

The son had always been aware of the importance of his own journey, but his father had also taught him to recognise the value of the journeys of others. His father's wisdom emphasised that life was not just about walking one's own path but also about helping those who struggled along the way. By lending a hand and walking alongside those who faced difficulties, the son could share in their journey and contribute to their growth while also finding a deeper sense of purpose in his own.

His father had taught him that every person's journey was unique, with its own challenges and triumphs. Yet, there was wisdom in recognising the common threads that connected these journeys. The son learned that by offering compassion and support, he could help others move forward, even when their paths seemed steep or uncertain. This shared experience not only strengthened those he helped but also enriched his own understanding of the world and his place within it.

The son understood that wisdom was not just about personal growth but about the connections we make with others along the way. His father's teachings encouraged him to approach life with a spirit of empathy and collaboration, recognising that the journey was not meant to be walked alone. By supporting others, he could discover new strengths within himself and build bonds that would last a lifetime.

As he reflected on his father's words, the son realised that the true measure of his journey was not just in the distance he travelled but in the lives he touched along the way. His father's wisdom had guided him to see that by sharing the journey with others, he could create a legacy of kindness, understanding, and mutual support. This was the path that would lead not only to his own fulfillment but to the enrichment of all those who walked beside him.

Sharing the Wealth - 65

Son, share the pebbles that fade away,
The fleeting treasures that won't long stay.
Give freely of what cannot last,
And let their worth not be surpassed.

Store the wealth that endures through time,
The lasting gems that you can claim as mine.
For if you hoard what's meant to be shared,
The value of your wealth will not be spared.

In giving, you find the true gain,
And what remains will not be in vain.
So balance the gifts that you bestow,
And in your heart, let wisdom grow.

Reflection 65: Sharing the Wealth

The son had often pondered the concept of wealth and how best to manage it. His father had always emphasised the importance of not just accumulating wealth but also understanding the nature of what was truly valuable. His father's wisdom had taught him that not all treasures were meant to be kept; some were fleeting and should be shared with others, while others held enduring value and should be preserved with care.

His father had advised him to give freely of the pebbles that fade away, recognising that these temporary treasures, though precious in the moment, would not last forever. By sharing them, the son could ensure that their worth was not lost but rather multiplied through the act of giving. His father's teachings had instilled in him the understanding that wealth was not just about what one kept but also about what one shared with others.

The son learned that true wealth was found in the balance between giving and preserving. While it was important to store the lasting gems that could endure through time, it was equally important to recognise when to share what was meant to be shared. His father's wisdom had guided him to see that hoarding wealth, especially that which was meant to be given, could diminish its value. In contrast, sharing wealth brought true gain, enriching not only those who received but also the ones who gave.

As he reflected on his father's words, the son realised that the act of giving was not just a moral duty but a way to ensure that the wealth he had accumulated had a lasting impact. By balancing his gifts with wisdom, he could create a legacy of generosity and purpose. His father's teachings had shown him that in giving, he could find true fulfilment, and the wealth that remained with him would not be in vain but would continue to grow in significance.

Stay True to Your Path - 66

Son, some begin with a king's desire,
Seeking wealth in realms that never tire.
Their journey's path is not like yours,
They focus on gold and kingdom doors.

Others dream grandly from the start,
But in those dreams, they lose their heart.
They walk the road with vision blurred,
Chasing shadows, and wisdom unheard.

Keep your distance, stay aware,
For your journey holds treasures rare.
Gather your pebbles, one by one,
Don't be a guardian for another's run.

Your path is yours, to walk and own.
Let your wisdom and strength be shown
In every step, let truth prevail,
And let your journey tell its tale.

Reflection 66: Stay True to Your Path

The son had often observed how others around him seemed driven by grand ambitions, chasing after wealth and power with relentless determination. His father had always encouraged him to recognise the difference between his own journey and the paths of others. His father's wisdom emphasised that not all journeys were the same and that it was important to stay true to one's own path, focusing on the treasures that truly mattered.

His father had taught him that some people began their journeys with a desire for wealth and influence, seeking to build empires and amass fortunes. Others dreamed grandly but often lost their way, their vision blurred by the pursuit of goals that did not align with their true selves. The son learned that it was easy to be drawn into the ambitions of others, but his father's teachings had instilled in him the importance of maintaining his own course.

The son understood that his journey was unique, filled with treasures that were personal and meaningful to him. His father had advised him to gather his achievements and wisdom one by one, not as a guardian of someone else's ambitions but as a seeker of his own truth. By staying true to his path, the son could ensure that his journey was guided by integrity and purpose, rather than by the fleeting desires of others.

As he reflected on his father's words, the son realized that the key to a fulfilling journey was staying focused on his own goals and values. His father's wisdom had taught him that in every step, truth should prevail, and that the journey itself was a reflection of his inner strength and wisdom. By staying true to his path, the son could walk with confidence, knowing that his journey was his own to walk and own, and that it would tell a tale of purpose and fulfillment.

The Value of Your Journey - 67

Son, some may try to compensate,
For the hard work and the steps you take.
But your journey's not for sale or trade,
It's a glory that you alone have made.

They'll offer you gold, or words so grand,
To take your path from your own hand.
But what you've earned through sweat and strife,
Is the treasure of your very life.

Don't let them barter what's deeply yours,
For they're trading with your soul's own stores.
Hold fast to the journey that you've begun,
For the glory is yours when the day is done.

Reflection 67: The Value of Your Journey

The son had often encountered those who admired his journey, recognising the effort and determination it had taken for him to reach where he was. His father had always reminded him that the value of his journey was something deeply personal, something that could not be measured by external rewards or praise. His father's wisdom had taught him that while others might try to compensate or flatter him, the true worth of his journey was beyond any trade or bargain.

His father had warned him that there would be those who would offer gold or grand words, attempting to take his path from his hands. The son learned that these offers, though tempting, were not worth the sacrifice of the personal glory he had earned through his own sweat and strife. His journey was not for sale, for it was the culmination of his life's efforts, a treasure that belonged solely to him.

The son understood that the journey he had undertaken was more than just a series of steps; it was the very essence of his life's work. His father's teachings had instilled in him the importance of holding fast to what he had begun, recognising that the journey's true value lay in the personal growth and fulfilment it brought. By staying true to his path, the son could ensure that the glory of his achievements remained his own, untarnished by the offers of others.

As he reflected on his father's words, the son realised that the journey was not just about reaching a destination, but about the process itself. His father's wisdom had guided him to see that the value of his journey was not something to be traded or diminished, but something to be cherished and protected. By honouring the path he had walked, the son could continue to find meaning and purpose in every step, knowing that the glory of his journey was his alone to hold.

Travel with those whose thoughts align,
In their company, let wisdom shine.
Talk with them as you journey through,
Learn and gain from their experience too.

Observe the pebbles they've amassed,
Perhaps you've missed some as you passed.
Collect the gems that your path may lack,
And add their treasures to your track.

For in each step and shared delight,
New insights bloom and guide your sight.
Embrace the journey with open heart,
And gather the wisdom others impart.

Reflection 68: Gathering Along the Way

The son had often walked his path with a sense of determination, focused on his own journey and the lessons he had learned along the way. But his father had always reminded him of the importance of not travelling alone. His father's wisdom emphasised the value of sharing the journey with others whose thoughts and values aligned with his own, recognising that there was much to be gained from the experiences and insights of those around him.

His father had encouraged him to engage in meaningful conversations with those he met on his journey, to talk with them and learn from their wisdom. The son learned that by observing the pebbles others had amassed—their experiences, insights, and the lessons they had gathered—he could enrich his own path. His father's teachings had instilled in him the understanding that there were treasures to be found in the journeys of others, treasures that could fill gaps in his own knowledge and guide him more effectively.

The son understood that the journey was not just about personal growth but also about the collective wisdom that could be shared and gathered along the way. His father's advice had taught him to embrace the journey with an open heart, to be receptive to the insights and experiences of others. By doing so, he could gather new treasures, adding to the wealth of knowledge and understanding that would help him navigate the road ahead.

As he reflected on his father's words, the son realised that the journey was made richer by the company of others. His father's wisdom had shown him that by travelling with those whose thoughts aligned with his, he could not only learn from their experiences but also contribute to their growth. Together, they could create a tapestry of wisdom, each thread adding strength and colour to the path they walked. The son knew that in each step and shared delight, new insights would bloom, guiding him and those around him toward a brighter future.

Balancing the Journey - 69

Son, understand this truth profound,
The path is the same, the distance is bound.
Pebbles are scattered along the way,
Not how fast you reach, but how you sway.

Balance your journey with mindful grace,
Collecting pebbles at your own pace.
Share your stories, exchange your views,
Leave behind wisdom that others may use.

The difference lies in how you balance,
The pain and pleasure, the steady dance.
Hard work and sacrifice, friends and foes,
Rest and toil in the life you chose.

In this balance, your achievements are found,
Not in speed, but in how you're crowned.
So tread the path with wisdom keen,
In every step, let your journey be seen.

Reflection 69: Balancing the Journey

The son had often heard stories of those who raced through life, focused on reaching their goals as quickly as possible. But his father had always taught him a different approach. His father's wisdom emphasised that the journey was not just about how fast one could reach the destination but about the balance one maintained along the way. It was in this balance that true fulfilment and wisdom were found.

His father had explained that the path was the same for everyone, with the same distance to travel. However, the difference lay in how each person balanced the experiences they encountered. The son learned that life was not a race but a journey where the careful collection of wisdom, the sharing of stories, and the exchange of views were just as important as the final destination. His father's teachings had instilled in him the understanding that every step, every pebble gathered, was part of a larger mosaic that made up the story of his life.

The son understood that balancing the journey meant navigating the challenges and joys with equal grace. His father had taught him to balance hard work and sacrifice with rest and reflection, to manage relationships with friends and foes, and to find harmony in the dance of life. It was in this balance that his achievements would be truly meaningful, not because of the speed at which he reached them but because of the thoughtful and intentional way he had walked his path.

As he reflected on his father's words, the son realised that the journey was not just about the destination but about how he lived each moment along the way. His father's wisdom had guided him to see that success was not measured by how quickly he reached his goals but by how well he balanced the many aspects of his life. In every step, the son found the opportunity to let his journey be seen, to share the wisdom he had gathered, and to leave behind a legacy of balance and grace.

Pam's feedback is thoughtful and her suggestions refine the flow and meaning of the poem. Here's a revised version incorporating her ideas:

He ran to his bed and snatched his diary,
In moments, slumber would seize him, though weary.
Glancing at the to-do list, he ticked with resolve,
Setting it aside, yet a storm did evolve.

His life's not been seamless, a turbulent sea,
With insecurities, projects that wouldn't quite be.
Failures, near misses, memories old,
Swirled in chaos around him, dark stories retold.

As he lay, his mind played a harrowing reel,
Of sleepless nights, of fears that won't heal.
Worrying over deadlines, disappointing the dear,
Haunted by echoes of past mistakes, near.

A perfectionist's chase, relentless, unkind,
Yet success remained distant, eluding his mind.
Projects that faltered, chances missed close,
Anxiety stormed, an unending dose.

Tonight, a small triumph in his nightly routine,
Ticking off tasks gave him a brief, soothing sheen.
A new habit forming, solace in the pall,
Acknowledging progress, though it might seem small.

Eyes closed, he yearned for a calm, gentle night,
Learning to still his mind, to silence the fright.
Drifting to dreams with a fragile, soft hope,
That peace might come, a way to cope.

In the night-time dark, he whispered a vow,
To embrace life's imperfections as of now.
To forget past failings, celebrate wins slight,
Tonight he would rest, dawn brings new light.

Reflection 70: The Weight of Sleepless Nights

The son had often found himself overwhelmed by the pressures of his own expectations, a relentless pursuit of perfection that left him sleepless and anxious. His father had always emphasised the importance of balance and self-compassion, but the son struggled to apply these lessons in the face of mounting deadlines, missed opportunities, and the weight of his own insecurities.

Each night, as he lay in bed, his mind would replay the day's events in a harrowing reel, bringing to the surface memories of past failures and near misses. The to-do lists that he meticulously crafted each morning became a source of both solace and torment, as the unchecked tasks seemed to mock him, reminding him of the perfection he had yet to achieve.

His life felt like a turbulent sea, filled with projects that didn't quite reach fruition, and insecurities that refused to be quieted. The son knew that this pursuit of perfection was unkind, yet he couldn't escape the anxiety that stormed within him, a ceaseless dose of worry that left him exhausted but unable to rest.

Yet, in the midst of this turmoil, there were moments of small triumphs—ticking off tasks on his list, forming new habits, and finding solace in the small progress he made each day. These moments, though fleeting, offered him a brief respite, a soothing sheen in the otherwise stormy night.

His father's teachings had always encouraged him to embrace life's imperfections, to forgive past failings, and to celebrate even the smallest of wins. The son realised that the weight of sleepless nights could be lifted if only he could learn to still his mind and silence the fears that haunted him.

As he closed his eyes, he made a vow to himself—a whispered promise to embrace imperfection, to find peace in the small victories, and to let go of the relentless chase for perfection. Tonight, he would rest, for dawn would bring new light and new opportunities to grow, learn, and continue his journey.

The Quiet Undercurrent - 71

In a world of flashing lights and fame,
Where headlines scream and vie for name,
We chase the glimmer, loud and bright,
Yet miss the whispers in the night.

For life is not in glitter's glare,
Nor in the crowns that few may wear,
But in the flow, the steady stream,
The quiet force that feeds our dream.

Beneath the noise, beneath the show,
An undercurrent, deep and slow,
Moves unseen, with gentle grace,
Carving paths through time and space.

It doesn't shout, it doesn't boast,
But nurtures all we cherish most—
The bonds that grow with love and care,
The wisdom that's beyond compare.

Like rivers winding through the land,
It shapes us with a subtle hand,
Guiding us through joy and strife,
Teaching the quiet truths of life.

So let us honour what we feel,
The silent strength that's ever real,
And find our power, deep within,
Where life's true currents gently spin.

For in the depths, we come to see,
The quiet flow that sets us free,
Not in the noise, but in the calm,
We find our path, our truth, our psalm.

Reflection 71: The Quiet Undercurrent

The son had often been drawn to the flashing lights of success, the allure of fame, and the noise of achievement that seemed to dominate the world around him. His father had always cautioned him against being blinded by these distractions, reminding him that the true essence of life was not found in the glitter and glamour, but in the quiet, steady forces that shaped his journey.

His father had spoken of the quiet undercurrent, a subtle but powerful force that moved beneath the surface of life. It was not loud or boastful, but it nurtured everything that truly mattered—the bonds of love and care, the wisdom that guided his steps, and the deep connections that sustained him through both joy and strife. The son learned that this undercurrent was the true source of strength, shaping his path with gentle grace and guiding him through the complexities of life.

The son understood that while the world often celebrated the loud and the bright, it was the quiet undercurrent that held the most profound truths. His father's teachings had instilled in him the value of looking beyond the noise, of finding peace and purpose in the calm, steady flow of life. The son realized that true power came not from chasing fame or fortune, but from embracing the quiet force that nurtured his dreams and sustained his spirit.

As he reflected on his father's words, the son recognized the importance of honouring the quiet undercurrent that ran through his life. It was in this quiet flow that he found his true path, his deepest strength, and the wisdom to navigate the challenges that lay ahead. His father's wisdom had guided him to see that life's most important currents were often unseen, but they were the ones that truly set him free, helping him to discover his own truth and purpose.

The Ships We Build – 72

Families pass down values, deep,
Like anchors in the soul, they keep.
Generations hold the tales,
Of love and loss, of winds and sails.

They cherish stories, old and wise,
The kind that opens hearts and eyes.
In times of joy, in times of pain,
They gather close, like drops of rain.

Together, they withstand the storm,
And keep each other safe and warm.
They build the ships that sail through life,
And mend the ones worn down by strife.

With hands that work and hearts that care,
They fix the broken, make it fair.
For in the bonds that families weave,
There lies the strength to dream, believe.

And so they sail, through calm and squall,
Supporting each, embracing all.
The ships they build, the tales told,
Become the legacy they hold.

Reflection 72: The Ships We Build

The son had always been aware of the deep values that his family had passed down through generations. His father had often spoken of these values as anchors for the soul, grounding each member of the family in love, wisdom, and resilience. The stories told around the dinner table, the lessons learned through shared experiences, and the bonds forged in times of both joy and pain were the building blocks of the family's legacy.

His father had taught him that families were like ships, crafted with care and attention to detail, designed to navigate the turbulent waters of life. Each generation contributed to the construction of these ships, adding their own experiences, wisdom, and strength to the vessel. The son learned that it was through the collective efforts of the family that these ships were able to sail through calm seas and weather the fiercest storms.

The son understood that the ships they built were not just physical constructs but representations of the love, support, and resilience that defined their family. His father's teachings had instilled in him the importance of mending the ships when they were worn down by strife, of working together to ensure that no member of the family was left adrift. The son realised that the bonds they wove together were the true strength of the family, enabling them to dream, believe, and sail forward with confidence.

As he reflected on his father's words, the son recognised the significance of the legacy they were creating. The ships they built, the stories they told, and the values they upheld would continue to guide future generations, providing them with the tools and strength needed to navigate their own journeys. His father's wisdom had shown him that the family's legacy was not just in the material possessions they passed down but in the enduring bonds of love and support that would carry them through life's challenges.

The Tapestry of Life - 73

We see the threads of love and pain,
The breakups, misunderstandings' stain,
Success we cheer, failure we embrace,
For each has its own time and place.

Yet some will dance in failure's light,
And frown at triumph's gleaming sight,
For in their eyes, the world is spun,
Where loss and gain are never one.

It's not just luck that guides our way,
But efforts made, day by day,
Abilities honed through trial and strife,
That carve the path we walk in life.

The loved ones may not win it all,
Nor do the hated always fall,
For life's a game of twists and turns,
Where every heart both wins and burns.

In victories sweet and losses deep,
We find the truths we choose to keep,
For in the dance of joy and tears,
We learn to conquer all our fears.

So let us walk this winding road,
With love and wisdom as our code,
For in the end, it's not the prize,
But how we lived and grew so wise.

Reflection 73: The Tapestry of Life

The son had come to realize that life was a complex tapestry, woven with threads of love, pain, success and failure. His father had always encouraged him to see the beauty in this intricate design, understanding that each thread, no matter how bright or dark, contributed to the overall picture of his life. The tapestry was not simply a matter of luck or chance; it was shaped by the efforts made, the abilities honed, and the lessons learned through the trials and triumphs along the way.

His father had taught him that life was full of contrasts—moments of joy and sorrow, success and failure, love and misunderstanding. These contrasts were not to be feared or avoided but embraced as part of the human experience. The son learned that it was in these moments, both high and low, that he found the truths that would guide him forward. His father's wisdom had instilled in him the importance of facing life's challenges with courage and grace, knowing that each experience added to the richness of his journey.

The son understood that life was not about winning or losing, but about how he chose to live and grow through each experience. His father had reminded him that victories and losses were both part of the same dance, teaching him to conquer his fears and embrace the fullness of life. The son realized that the true measure of his life was not in the prizes he won, but in the wisdom he gained and the love he shared along the way.

As he reflected on his father's words, the son recognized the importance of walking the winding road of life with love and wisdom as his guiding principles. His father's teachings had shown him that the tapestry of life was not just a collection of experiences, but a work of art that he created through his choices, actions, and the way he embraced each moment. In the end, the son knew that it was not the destination that mattered most, but the journey itself and the wisdom he gained along the way.

Tales of Shadows and Light - 74

The unsuccessful tell their tale,
Of others too, who fear they'll fail.
Some change the story, twist the plot,
And judge what's real and what is not.

Families weave their tales so strange,
With threads of truth, they rearrange.
Imagination spreads its wings,
Creating myths of wondrous things.

Creativity takes the lead,
In stories born of whispered need.
In the end, we bear the names,
Of all that's built, of all the blames.

Yet our families stay close and near,
Supporting us through doubt and fear.
Though some may hide what's not disclosed,
Their love remains, though not exposed.

We hide our lives like the sun,
Behind the clouds when the day is done,
Or mountains high that block the light,
But always there, just out of sight.

In shadows cast, in light that fades,
We live our lives in many shades,
Yet through it all, the ties remain,
Binding us through joy and pain.

Reflection 74: Tales of Shadows and Light

The son had always been fascinated by the stories that families told, stories that blended truth with imagination, shaping their identities and their understanding of the world. His father had often spoken of these tales, acknowledging that they were not always straightforward or entirely true. Families, in their attempt to make sense of their experiences, often wove narratives that mixed reality with fiction, creating myths that were passed down through generations.

His father had taught him that these stories were a reflection of the human need to explain, to justify and to connect. They were born out of whispered needs, out of the desire to create meaning from the events of life. The son learned that while some stories were told with clarity and honesty, others were twisted or rearranged, hiding certain truths or emphasising certain perspectives. Yet, through it all, the stories served a purpose, binding the family together even as they navigated the shadows and light of their shared experiences.

The son understood that every family had its own tales of success and failure, of joy and pain. His father had reminded him that these stories, whether entirely true or partly imagined, were part of the fabric of the family's identity. They were the threads that connected them, even when the light of truth was partially obscured by the shadows of doubt and fear.

As he reflected on his father's words, the son realized that the stories his family told were not just about the past, but about their hopes and fears for the future. His father's wisdom had guided him to see that while some truths were hidden and some tales were altered, the love and support of the family remained constant. In the end, it was the ties that bound them together through all the shadows and light that truly mattered, shaping their collective journey and their shared destiny.

The Crossroads of Love and Success - 75

Parents stand at crossroads wide,
Where love, success both coincide,
Feeling the weight of choices made,
In the tender balance of love's parade.

Some push their children toward the heights,
Chasing dreams through days and nights,
Believing that success will show
The depth of love they wish to bestow.

Others hold their children near,
Guarding them from worldly fear,
Choosing warmth over ambition's call,
Finding success in love's gentle thrall.

With every step, each choice they weigh,
Guided by their own life's sway,
They start with hopes, with dreams imbued,
And navigate the path they've viewed.

Love and success, they intertwine,
In every choice, both yours and mine,
Parents begin with hearts sincere,
Facing a journey both bright and clear.

In the end, the bond remains,
Through struggles and doubts, joys, and pains,
For in each choice, each gentle shove,
Is the echo of a parent's love.

Reflection 75: The Crossroads of Love and Success

The son often reflected on the choices his parents had made throughout his life, recognising the delicate balance they had to strike between love and success. His father had spoken to him many times about the crossroads that every parent faces—the point at which they must decide how to guide their children, whether to push them toward achievement or to hold them close, offering protection and warmth.

His father had taught him that these choices were not easy, and each parent made them based on their own experiences, hopes, and fears. Some parents, driven by their desire for their children to succeed, would encourage them to chase their dreams relentlessly, believing that success was the ultimate expression of their love. Others, however, chose to prioritize emotional closeness, shielding their children from the harsh realities of the world and finding fulfilment in the love and security they provided.

The son understood that his parents' decisions were made with the best of intentions, guided by the values they held dear. His father had always emphasised that love and success were not mutually exclusive, but rather intertwined in complex ways. Every choice made by a parent was influenced by their own journey, their own struggles, and their own dreams for their children.

As he reflected on his father's words, the son realised that, despite the different paths parents might choose, the bond of love was the constant thread that connected them. His father's wisdom had shown him that, in the end, it was not the specific choices that mattered most, but the love that

guided those choices. Through struggles, doubts, joys, and
pains, the love of a parent was always present, shaping the
journey and strengthening the bond between parent and
child.

The Relatives' Watch – 76

Relatives watch the families play,
Making their choices in their own way.
They form their groups, both near and far,
Guided by each life's distinctive scar.

Some gather in the realm of success,
Admiring feats that impress and bless.
While others dwell in the gossip's flow,
Weaving tales where whispers grow.

They share their feelings, craft their tales,
Judging each choice as time prevails.
Though their scrutiny may seem unkind,
They are the kind you cannot leave behind.

Unlike friends or colleagues, you may trade,
These are the bonds that never fade.
Stay close, yet keep a measured space,
Navigating each familiar face.

For in their presence, both warmth and strain,
Lies a connection that will remain.
Keep them near, but with a careful hand,
In the ebb and flow of this family land.

Reflection 76: The Relatives' Watch

The son had always been aware of the watchful eyes of his relatives, those family members who, from near and far, observed the lives of their kin with a mixture of curiosity, judgment, and affection.

His father had often spoken to him about the complex dynamics that existed within the extended family, reminding him that while friends and colleagues might come and go, relatives were a permanent part of one's life.

His father had taught him that relatives formed their own groups, guided by their unique experiences, scars, and perceptions. Some gathered in admiration of success, celebrating the achievements of those who had risen to prominence. Others, however, found solace in the flow of gossip, weaving tales that sometimes twisted the truth and magnified the flaws of others.

The son learned that these observations and judgments, though sometimes unkind, were part of the fabric of family life. The son understood that relatives, with their differing perspectives and opinions, played a significant role in shaping the family narrative.

His father had advised him to stay close to his relatives but to also maintain a measured distance, navigating each relationship with care.

The son realised that these bonds, though sometimes challenging, were unbreakable and required careful management to maintain harmony within the family.

As he reflected on his father's words, the son recognised the dual nature of his relationships with his relatives. There was warmth and support, but also strain and tension, as each relative brought their own perspective to the table.

His father's wisdom had shown him that the key to navigating these relationships was to keep them close but, with a careful hand, balance the need for connection with the need for personal space. In this way, the son could honour the enduring bonds of family while maintaining his own sense of self within the larger familial landscape.

The Dance of Friendship - 77

Friends are varied, far and wide,
Some drift away, some stay beside.
They come and go, a shifting tide,
Yet in their midst, we often confide.

Conversations start where they last left off,
Whether it's yesterday or a year's soft.
The topics, though old, feel fresh anew,
In their company, ideas renew.

In the ebb and flow of friendship's grace,
We find our growth, our own embrace.
One friend or many, the circle spins,
Each one adds to the journey within.

Through shared dreams and moments deep,
In laughter and tears, in silence we keep,
It's with these friends that we truly grow,
Finding ourselves in the stories we sow.

Reflection 77: The Dance of Friendship

The son had always cherished the friendships he had formed over the years, recognising the unique role they played in his life. His father had often spoken of the dynamic nature of friendships, how they ebbed and flowed like the tides, with some friends drifting away and others remaining steadfast by his side. These relationships, though varied, were essential to his growth and self-discovery.

His father had taught him that true friendship was not defined by constant presence but by the ability to pick up where they last left off, whether it had been days, months, or even years. The son learned that in the company of friends, ideas were renewed, and old topics could feel fresh and invigorating. These conversations, no matter how long the gap, were a source of inspiration and reflection.

The son understood that the dance of friendship was a journey in itself, with each friend adding to the richness of his experiences. His father had emphasised the importance of embracing this dance, recognising that through shared dreams, moments of laughter, and even the silent understanding of shared struggles, friendships helped him to grow in ways he could not have achieved alone.

As he reflected on his father's words, the son realised that the circle of friends he had formed over the years was a vital part of his life's journey. His father's wisdom had shown him that it was through these connections that he found himself learning from the stories they shared and the experiences they lived together. In the dance of friendship, the son discovered not only the joy of companionship but also the deeper understanding of himself and the world around him.

Success from the Unknown – 78

Success often springs from places unseen,
From sources unknown, where you've not been.
Those you've never known, and you never sought,
Shape plans around you, in ways untaught.

In these moments, your true self will shine,
As you work to prove what is truly thine.
No judgments from friends or relatives near,
Just pure opportunity, clear and sincere.

They don't dwell on your tales or past mistakes,
Instead, they offer chances that success makes.
They challenge you to grow and rise,
To reach beyond the familiar skies.

Here, the opportunities stretch far and wide,
Unfettered by the past, with nothing to hide.
Embrace these paths, let your spirit soar,
For success often comes from the unknown door.

Reflection 78: Success from the Unknown

The son had always been aware of the power of familiarity—
the comfort of being surrounded by those who knew him
well, who understood his past, and who shared in his
successes and failures. But his father had also taught him to
recognise the potential that lay beyond the familiar, in the
unknown opportunities that life could present. These were
the moments where true success often emerged, from places
unseen and sources unknown.

His father had spoken to him about the importance of
embracing these opportunities, especially when they came
from those who had no preconceived notions of who he was
or what he could achieve. These were the people who did not
judge him based on his past, who did not dwell on his
mistakes, but instead saw the potential for success that lay
within him. The son learned that in these moments, his true
self could shine, free from the limitations of previous
judgments and expectations.

The son understood that success often came from the
unknown—those doors that opened unexpectedly, offering
new paths that stretched far and wide. His father had
emphasised that these opportunities were not to be feared but
embraced, for they held the potential to propel him to new
heights. It was in these unfamiliar spaces that he could truly
grow, reaching beyond the boundaries of what he had known
and exploring new horizons.

As he reflected on his father's words, the son realized that
the key to success was not just in mastering the familiar, but
in stepping into the unknown with courage and confidence.
His father's wisdom had guided him to see that the unknown
was not a place of uncertainty, but a realm of infinite
possibilities. By embracing these opportunities, the son

knew he could achieve success in ways he had never imagined, guided by the belief that the unknown often held the greatest potential for growth and achievement.

The Guiding Light of Teachers – 79

Teachers stand as beacons bright,
In classrooms and beyond, they guide our sight.
Through the pages of books, they lead the way,
Unveiling themes and meanings day by day.

They see the world through varied views,
And in their gaze, they find the hues
Of potential and growth, both near and far,
Shaping who we'll be, like sculptors of a star.

They guide us through the labyrinth of thought,
Helping us find the lessons sought.
Their wisdom is a treasure, deeply sewn,
In every lesson, in every tone.

Keep them close, these mentors true,
For in their presence, you'll find a clue.
Meet them often, share your dreams,
In their guidance, strength redeems.

They polish our edges, refine our core,
Opening paths to learn and explore.
With their help, we grow and shine,
In the light of their knowledge, we align.

Reflection 79: The Guiding Light of Teachers

The son had always held a deep respect for the teachers who had guided him throughout his life. His father had often spoken of the profound impact that teachers could have, not just within the walls of a classroom but in shaping the very course of a student's journey. Teachers were more than just educators; they were beacons of light, guiding their students through the complexities of knowledge, thought and life itself.

His father had taught him that teachers saw the world through varied lenses, each bringing a unique perspective that helped to shape the minds of those they taught. The son learned that in the gaze of a teacher, potential and growth were recognized, nurtured, and brought to fruition. His father had always described teachers as sculptors, patiently refining the rough edges of their students, helping them to shine like stars in their own right.

The son understood that the lessons imparted by his teachers were treasures, deeply woven into the fabric of his being.

His father had emphasised the importance of keeping these mentors close, of meeting with them often and sharing dreams and aspirations.

It was through the guidance of these teachers that the son found strength, clarity, and direction in his life.

As he reflected on his father's words, the son realised that the wisdom of his teachers had not only helped him navigate the labyrinth of thought but had also opened up new paths of exploration and discovery.

His father's teachings had shown him that teachers were instrumental in helping students align their inner potential with the world around them. By refining their knowledge, polishing their understanding, and guiding them with care, teachers played a crucial role in helping their students grow and shine.

The Dance with Neighbours – 80

Neighbours, seen yet unknown by name,
They watch the dance of fortune's game.
Though they know little of your life's own thread,
They measure wealth by the outward spread.

In their gaze, you find comparison's spark,
Reflecting in the shadows, both light and dark.
Stay around, observe the ebb and flow,
But let their success not cast your glow.

You build from what you have, not what they claim,
Avoiding the trap of the comparison game.
Let their achievements be their own,
And let your path remain unknown.

In quiet play, from a distance far,
You navigate beneath your own guiding star.
Match their steps, or surpass with grace,
But let not envy mar your place.

For in this dance, both near and wide,
Success is shaped by the inner tide.
Play your game with calm and poise,
Embrace your journey, find your own voice.

Reflection 80: The Dance with Neighbours

The son had always been aware of the presence of his neighbours, those familiar faces seen day in and day out, yet often unknown by name or story. His father had often spoken about the subtle dance that occurred between neighbours—the observations, the comparisons, and the silent judgments that were part of living in close proximity. While neighbours might know little of each other's inner lives, they often measured success by the outward signs, by the visible markers of wealth, status, and fortune.

His father had taught him the importance of being mindful of this dance, recognising the natural tendency to compare oneself to others. The son learned that while it was easy to get caught up in the successes or failures of those around him, it was crucial to remain focused on his own path, to build from what he had, rather than from what others claimed. His father had emphasised that true success was not about surpassing others but about staying true to one's own journey, guided by an inner sense of purpose and direction.

The son understood that in this dance with neighbours, it was important to observe and learn but not to let comparison dictate his actions or cloud his judgment. His father's wisdom had guided him to see that each person's achievements were their own and that his own path, though different, was equally valid. The son realised that by navigating his life with calm and poise; by embracing his own journey, he could find his voice and create his own success, free from the shadows of envy or competition.

As he reflected on his father's words, the son recognised that the dance with neighbours was not just about external appearances, but about the inner tide that shaped his decisions and actions. His father had shown him that true success was a personal journey, one that required a steady hand and a clear vision, untainted by the noise of comparison. By embracing his own path, the son knew he could play the game of life with grace and confidence, secure in the knowledge that his success was his own to define.

The Seasons Within - 81

Within yourself, no different, you remain,
Like seasons shifting through joy and pain.
Your moods, like weather, rise and fall,
From high to low, through it all.

You're at once a friend and stranger too,
A relative or neighbour, as you renew.
In the mirror of your mind's own grace,
You shift between roles in your inner space.

The seasons change, and so do you,
Embracing the old and the new.
Through every mood and every phase,
You navigate life's intricate maze.

Yet through these fluctuations, clear and true,
You're always the same, just evolving you.
Embrace the changes with each passing day,
For in this journey, you find your way.

Reflection 81: The Seasons Within

The son had always been fascinated by the way his emotions and moods seemed to change with the ebb and flow of life. His father had often spoken of these internal shifts, comparing them to the changing seasons—each with its own character, its own influence, yet all part of the same cycle of life. The son learned that, just as the weather changes from day to day, so too did his internal landscape, with highs and lows that were as natural as the seasons themselves.

His father had taught him that within each person, there existed a multitude of roles and faces—a friend, a stranger, a relative, or a neighbour—all reflections of the same core self. These roles shifted and changed with the circumstances of life, yet through it all, the son remained true to his essence, continuously evolving as he navigated the complexities of his inner world.

The son understood that these fluctuations in mood and perspective were not something to fear or resist, but to embrace as part of the journey. His father had emphasised the importance of accepting these changes, recognising that they were all part of the intricate maze of life. Each phase, each mood, brought with it lessons and insights that helped to shape the person he was becoming.

As he reflected on his father's words, the son realized that despite the changes he experienced, there was a constancy within him—a core self that remained, growing and evolving with each passing day. His father's wisdom had guided him to see that the journey of life was not just about the external experiences but about the internal seasons that shaped his understanding of the world and himself. By embracing these changes, the son knew he could find his way, navigating life's twists and turns with a sense of purpose and grace.

The Exchange of Roles – 82

In shifting roles, where friends fade away,
And colleagues step into kin's display.
The lines once clear now blur and bend,
As what was familiar comes to an end.

A friend feels distant, where warmth once grew,
While a colleague's embrace feels strangely new.
These changing roles weave a tangled thread,
Where connection thins, and old ties shed.

Confusion reigns where clarity once lay,
As the dance of roles begins to sway.
You adjust your steps, seeking the flow,
In rhythms where old patterns go.

Yet through this shift, one truth remains,
To find the balance in what still sustains.
For in the ebb and flow of life's grand scroll,
Love unfolds in every changing role.

Reflection 82: The Exchange of Roles

The son had often found himself puzzled by the shifting dynamics of relationships in his life. His father had always spoken about the fluidity of roles, how friends could sometimes become distant, while colleagues might step into the warmth of family. These exchanges of roles, though natural, often left the son feeling disoriented, as the familiar became foreign and the lines that once seemed clear began to blur.

His father had taught him that life was a constant dance, where the steps were not always predictable, and the roles of those around him could change without warning. The son learned that these changes, while confusing, were part of the intricate tapestry of human connections. He understood that in this dance, it was important to remain adaptable, to realign his expectations and embrace the new rhythms that emerged.

The son recognised that these exchanges of roles were not just about the people around him, but also about his own ability to navigate the shifting landscape of relationships. His father had emphasised the importance of understanding the ebb and flow of these changes, to seek harmony even when the roles felt misaligned. The son realised that the heart's intent in these situations was to find balance, to maintain love and connection despite the shifting dynamics.

As he reflected on his father's words, the son understood that the key to navigating these changes was to remain open and flexible, to adjust his steps in the dance of life with grace and intention. His father's wisdom had guided him to see that while roles might change, the underlying connections could still thrive if approached with care and understanding. In this way, the son could continue to foster meaningful relationships, even as the roles evolved.

The Freshness and the Mess - 83

Exchanging roles brings a breath of fresh air,
A new perspective in the dance we share.
Friends become distant, and colleagues close,
In this shifting play where relationships transpose.

Yet, as time unfolds, the clarity wanes,
And what was fresh turns into tangled chains.
The novelty fades, and the mess remains,
As roles return to their familiar strains.

What once seemed new now feels askew,
The freshness brings a cluttered view.
In time, the roles reset, find their place,
And the dance resumes its accustomed grace.

Thus, while the change brings moments bright,
It often circles back to familiar light.
In the end, the roles you knew will stay,
As the freshness melds with the olden way.

Reflection 83: The Freshness and the Mess

The son had experienced first-hand the shifts in roles that could occur within relationships. His father had often spoken of the way these changes could bring a breath of fresh air, offering new perspectives and opportunities to see others in a different light. Friends who had grown distant might suddenly become closer, while colleagues could take on the warmth and familiarity of kin. These exchanges, though initially invigorating, brought with them a certain level of unpredictability.

His father had taught him that while these changes could be refreshing, they often came with their own set of challenges. The son learned that as time unfolded, the clarity that once accompanied the newness of these roles began to wane. What had once felt fresh and exciting could quickly turn into a tangled mess, with roles and relationships becoming muddled and confused. The novelty of these changes would often fade, leaving behind a sense of disarray as everyone struggled to find their footing once again.

The son understood that this cycle was a natural part of life's ebb and flow. His father had emphasised that while the exchange of roles could bring moments of brightness and renewal, it was also important to recognise when the mess outweighed the freshness. Over time, the roles would often reset, finding their way back to a more familiar and comfortable place. The son realized that in the end, these shifts, though valuable, were often temporary, and the relationships would eventually return to their original dynamics.

As he reflected on his father's words, the son recognised the importance of embracing these changes while also understanding their limits. His father's wisdom had guided him to see that while the freshness of role exchanges could bring new energy and perspective, it was essential to navigate the ensuing mess with patience and care. In this way, the son could appreciate the moments of change while also finding comfort in the stability that eventually followed.

The Rhythm of Routine – 84

Rise with the dawn, embrace the day's start,
With a moment to reflect, to calm the heart.
Clear your mind with purpose and grace,
Finding your balance, your own quiet space.

Release what's not worth carrying—**love or hate**,
Let go of the shadows that clutter your fate.
Avoid the tangles of unresolved past,
Create each day anew, fresh and steadfast.

Not everyone you know is worth your thought,
Be mindful of your time when it is sought.
Whether near or far, they weave through your day,
In the routine of life, let your own path stay.

Build each day with clarity, free from the weight,
Crafting moments of freshness, not bound by fate.
Embrace the routine, but let your spirit be free,
In the rhythm of living, find harmony.

Reflection 84: The Rhythm of Routine

The son had always found comfort in the routines that structured his days. His father had often spoken about the power of routine, how it could provide a sense of stability and purpose in an otherwise chaotic world. The son learned that by embracing the rhythm of routine, he could start each day with a clear mind and a calm heart, setting the tone for whatever challenges or opportunities might arise.

His father had taught him that routines were not just about repetition but about intention. The son understood that the key to a fulfilling routine was to approach each day with purpose, to release the burdens that were not worth carrying—whether they were unresolved conflicts, lingering regrets, or unnecessary worries. His father had emphasised the importance of letting go of the shadows that cluttered his life, allowing him to create each day anew with a sense of freshness and resolve.

The son realised that while routines helped to maintain order, they also required flexibility. His father had reminded him that not everyone around him shared the same thoughts or priorities, yet he often found himself spending time on things that didn't align with his own path. The son learned to navigate these interactions with grace, ensuring that his routine allowed for connection with others without losing sight of his own goals.

As he reflected on his father's words, the son understood that the rhythm of routine was not just about following a set pattern but about finding harmony in the balance between routine and spontaneity. His father's wisdom had guided him to see that by building each day with clarity and intention, he could craft moments of freshness and joy unbound by the constraints of fate. In this way, the son found peace in the rhythm of his life, embracing routine as a tool for both stability and growth.

Carrying the Day - 85

With dawn, I rise, no weight in hand,
No cart to pull through shifting sand.
The day is mine, the sky is clear,
No strings to bind, no ghost to fear.

For some, the echoes of the past
Linger long, their shadows cast.
Ancestors' dreams and silent calls,
Descendants' hopes, like ancient walls.

But I walk light, my steps my own,
No burdened past, no future loan.
To prove my worth in silent night,
I carry the stars, my only light.

Yet in my heart, I feel the thread,
The ties unseen, the words unsaid.
The weight of love, the strength it brings,
Not a burden, but the song it sings.

For in this dance of time and kin,
We prove our worth not by the din,
But by the quiet, steady grace
Of carrying day, our chosen pace.

So I'll walk free, but not alone,
With every breath, a seed is sown.
No cart to pull, yet still I know,
The path I carve is mine to show.

Reflection 85: Carrying the Day

Reflecting on his father's life and wisdom, the son sees in the poem "Carrying the Day" a powerful message about personal freedom and the weight of love and responsibility. His father often spoke of walking through life without the heavy burdens of the past or future weighing him down but rather finding strength in the present moment. The son now understands that this strength comes from more than mere independence; it is deeply rooted in the love and ties that connect generations.

Though his father walked his path with quiet dignity, the son knows that his father's journey wasn't without its invisible threads—the unseen forces of family, tradition, and the silent dreams of ancestors. Yet these were not burdens. His father carried them lightly, with grace and a deep sense of purpose. The poem reflects this sense of quiet responsibility, where love and legacy are not seen as weights but as sources of strength and meaning.

The son sees now that to carry the day is not about bearing burdens but about walking with purpose, guided by the subtle connections that shape us. His father's wisdom has taught him that true worth is found in the quiet grace of moving forward, forging a path that honours both the past and the future while remaining free in the present.

Books hold the seeds of thoughts anew,
Crafted by minds with visions true.
They are not just reflections of your own,
But realms where countless ideas have grown.

In pages, you'll find not just what you think,
But the essence of others, like a bridge to link.
They capture behaviours, characters, and scenes,
Of lives and worlds beyond our daily means.

Write down your thoughts as you delve within,
For in these exchanges, new insights begin.
Let books be your guide, your conversations' spark,
Illuminating paths that once were dark.

By immersing in their wisdom, old and new,
You shape your own self with a broader view.
In the company of pages, your mind will expand,
Building a personality by the author's hand.

Reflection 86: The Wisdom of Books

The son had always found solace and inspiration in the pages of books. His father had often spoken about the immense value that books held, not just as sources of knowledge but as gateways to new realms of thought and imagination. The son learned that books were more than mere reflections of his own ideas; they were the products of countless minds, each offering a unique perspective and insight into the world.

His father had taught him that within the pages of a book, one could find the essence of other lives, other worlds, and other ways of thinking. The son realised that by immersing himself in these written words, he was not just reading but engaging in a conversation with the authors, bridging the gap between his own experiences and the vastness of human thought. His father had emphasised the importance of writing down his thoughts as he read, capturing the new insights that emerged from these exchanges.

The son understood that books were more than just tools for learning; they were companions on the journey of life. His father had shown him that by allowing books to guide his thoughts and spark his imagination, he could illuminate paths that had once seemed dark and uncertain. The son realised that the wisdom contained within books, both old and new, could shape his personality and expand his understanding of the world.

As he reflected on his father's words, the son recognised the transformative power of books. His father's wisdom had guided him to see that through reading, he could grow not just in knowledge but in empathy and understanding. By engaging with the thoughts and experiences of others, he could build a broader, more nuanced view of the world, shaping his own identity in the process. In the company of books, the son found a lifelong companion, one that would continue to guide and inspire him on his journey.

The Architects of Thought – 87

As you turn each page, let your thoughts entwine,
With the wisdom and ideas that you find.
Books are mirrors, reflecting new light,
Unveiling the depths of your inner sight.

Seek those who inspire, whose talents are rare,
Those who make you think, those who make you care.
Creative geniuses, with visions so grand,
Shape the mundane with a masterful hand.

From stones they craft monuments tall and wise,
From blank canvases, they bring art to life's eyes.
Their gifts transform the ordinary to divine,
In their creations, the essence of art does shine.

Let their brilliance guide your own inner quest,
In the dance of ideas, find your own zest.
For in the dialogue between thought and art,
You'll discover the wonders that shape your heart.

Reflection 87: The Architects of Thought

The son had always been drawn to the works of those who possessed a rare and creative vision, the architects of thought who could transform the ordinary into something extraordinary. His father had often spoken about the importance of engaging with such minds, those who could inspire and challenge him to think deeper, to care more, and to see the world through a different lens. These creative geniuses, his father explained, had the power to shape not just art and literature, but the very way people perceived life itself.

His father had taught him that books were more than just a collection of words; they were mirrors reflecting new light, unveiling the depths of one's inner sight. The son learned that by seeking out those who could inspire him—those whose talents were rare and whose visions were grand—he could find the guidance he needed to pursue his own inner quest. His father had emphasised the importance of letting these brilliant minds guide his thoughts, helping him to discover new ideas and perspectives that could shape his understanding of the world.

The son understood that these architects of thought were not just artists or writers, but creators in every sense of the word. They were the ones who could take the mundane and elevate it to the divine, crafting monuments of wisdom from stones and bringing art to life from blank canvases. His father had shown him that by engaging with their work, he could find his own zest for life, discovering the wonders that lay within his own heart.

As he reflected on his father's words, the son realised that the dialogue between thought and art was a powerful tool for personal growth. His father's wisdom had guided him to see that in this dance of ideas, he could find inspiration and insight, allowing him to shape his own path with creativity and purpose. By immersing himself in the brilliance of these creative minds, the son knew he could build a richer, more meaningful life, one that was shaped by the wonders of art and thought.

The Unsung Hero - 88

So spoke the father through pages worn,
Words of wisdom, softly adorned.
The children read, their tears fell,
Uncovering tales they never could tell.

In his book, they found a soul profound,
A silent hero, where thoughts abound.
Unknown to them, his depth and might,
A force like currents, hidden from sight.

He stood steadfast through life's fierce fight,
His presence felt, though veiled from light.
Quiet yet powerful, his essence was clear,
A strength revealed through the words they held dear.

In his writings, they glimpsed his core,
The depth of his being, the quiet roar.
A hero unsung, with thoughts so deep,
In the currents of life, his legacy keeps.

Reflection 88: The Unsung Hero

The children had always known their father as a steady, reliable presence in their lives, but it wasn't until they delved into the pages of his writings that they truly began to understand the depth of his character. Their father had always been a man of few words, often allowing his actions to speak for him. Yet, as they read his journals and reflections, they uncovered a side of him they had never fully appreciated—a side that revealed him as a profound thinker, a quiet force of wisdom and strength.

Their father's words, softly adorned with the wisdom of a life well-lived, spoke volumes about the struggles and triumphs he had faced. In the margins of those worn pages, the children found traces of a soul that had remained hidden from them—a soul that had weathered life's storms with quiet resilience. Their father, though never one to seek the spotlight, had been a hero in his own right, navigating the currents of life with a depth of thought and strength of spirit that they had only now begun to grasp.

The children were moved to tears as they realised how much of their father's inner world had been kept from view. He had been a pillar of strength for them, yet they had never fully understood the magnitude of his influence. In his writings, they found a legacy of thought that revealed the true essence of who he was—a man of quiet power, whose presence had shaped their lives in ways they were only now beginning to appreciate.

As they continued to read, the children discovered the heroism that had been quietly woven into the fabric of their father's life. He had stood steadfast through life's fiercest battles, his strength revealed not in grand gestures but in the enduring wisdom and love he had imparted to them. Through his words, they came to see him as an unsung hero, a man whose legacy would continue to guide and inspire them long after he was gone.

The Quiet Achievers – 89

While many speak of dreams and plans,
Of ventures, goals, and life's demands,
Few turn their words to deeds so true,
And act with purpose, to see it through.

Some vow to climb, to shed their weight,
To quit old habits, to change their fate.
Yet, it's the quiet few who do,
Their actions speak where words are few.

They scale the heights, mend their soul,
In silence, they achieve their goal.
Salute these souls with quiet care,
For in their journey, they leave a footprint there.

Their paths may seem both tough and grand,
With silver linings in every strand.
Respect their quiet strength and might,
For undercurrents guide their fight.

Reflection 89: The Quiet Achievers

The son had often heard people speak of their dreams, ambitions, and plans for the future. His father had always reminded him that while many are eager to talk about what they hope to achieve, it is the quiet achievers who truly make a difference. These are the individuals who, rather than proclaiming their intentions, focus on turning their words into deeds, quietly working towards their goals with determination and purpose.

His father had taught him to recognise the value of silent perseverance, the kind that doesn't seek applause or recognition but is driven by inner strength and commitment. The son learned that while many may vow to change their lives, to climb new heights, or to break free from old habits, it is the quiet few who succeed. Their actions speak louder than words, and their achievements, though often unnoticed, are the result of steadfast effort and resilience.

The son understood that these quiet achievers were worthy of respect and admiration. His father had emphasised that their paths, though often difficult and demanding, were marked by a strength that was both tough and grand. The son realised that in the journey of these individuals, there were valuable lessons to be learned; lessons about the power of purposeful action, the importance of silent determination, and the quiet strength that guides them through life's challenges.

As he reflected on his father's words, the son recognised the importance of honouring these quiet achievers. They may not seek the spotlight, but their contributions are profound, and their success is a testament to the power of perseverance and silent resolve. His father's wisdom had guided him to see that in the undercurrents of their journey, there was a depth of character and a strength of spirit that deserved to be celebrated.

Against the Flow – 90

When education grants its chance to shine,
And organizations lay their roles in line,
Performance brings the ranks to grow,
Each move, a step, a game we know.

But when the board is cleared, pieces stored,
Do we restart, or search for more?
For in that pause, a question blooms—
Why return to olden rooms?

To redo, regain takes time and care,
Yet why return when new paths flare?
The flow behind, the flow ahead,
The future's voice is what is said.

Let not the past define your course,
Against the flow, find your true source.
For in the shift, the bold renew,
And winning comes in something new.

Reflection 90: Against the Flow

The son remembered his father's advice about life's many choices, especially the ones that go against the flow. His father had taught him that when the familiar paths no longer served him, it was time to embrace new directions, even if they felt uncertain. The chessboard of life often resets, but his father had always encouraged him to step beyond the game and forge new paths. It was not about repeating the same moves but seeking growth and renewal in the unknown. His father's words guided him to understand that the boldest actions come from following one's true course, even when it challenges the status quo. In this, the son found strength, trusting that stepping away from the familiar flow could bring the greatest rewards.

The Legacy of New Beginnings – 91

Brides enter our homes, with stories untold,
Carrying the past, both tender and bold.
They bring their memories, dear ones, and tears,
The laughter of youth, and the weight of their years.

Some faced hardships, their spirits worn thin,
Others knew joy, where love did begin.
Each brings their journey, the highs and the lows,
Building new roots where old branches grow.

In their past lies the strength, the wisdom they share,
A family's foundation, crafted with care.
Come what may, through thick and thin,
Their past forms the bedrock where new lives begin.

And as these stories blend and unite,
They kindle a fire, warm and bright.
In the hearth of the home, where new life begins,
Their legacy lives on, through thick and thin.

Reflection 91: The Legacy of New Beginnings

The son recalled the quiet wisdom his father had shared about the women who entered their lives, bringing with them untold stories and memories. His father had spoken of the strength these women carried, often forged from hardship, joy, and a past that shaped them. The son understood, through his father's words, that each new bride brought not just her presence but her legacy, weaving her journey into the family's fabric. His father had reminded him that this blending of stories formed the foundation for new lives and that honouring their past while welcoming them into the future was the key to building strong families. In this way, the son saw how the legacy of new beginnings took root in every family, sustained by the stories of those who joined it.

Foundations of a Shared Journey – 92

The groom steps forward, with a duty to bear,
Taking on the mantle, with a heart full of care.
Together with his bride, a new chapter unfolds,
Where traditions meet change, and new stories are told.

Grooms come with stories, with lives they've led,
Carrying dreams and the paths they've tread.
Their past is a journey, with triumphs and strife,
The echoes of days that shaped their life.

Sometimes new thoughts challenge the old,
Evolving beliefs as the future takes hold.
But in the balance of love, respect, and might,
They navigate the path from darkness to light.

Some knew struggle, with burdens to bear,
Others found fortune in love and care.
Each brings his tale, both the joy and the pain,
Building new ties where old bonds remain.

At times, values are questioned, or quietly set aside,
Yet through it all, their unity is their guide.
For in the blending of old and new, there lies a truth,
A family's foundation, shaped by both age and youth.

In his past lies the courage, the lessons he's learned,
A family's foundation, where respect is earned.
Come what may, in joy or in strife,
His past forms the bedrock of this shared new life.

Reflection 92: Foundations of a Shared Journey

The son had often heard his father speak of the responsibilities a man takes on when he enters marriage. His father had emphasised that this was not a solo journey but a shared one, where both husband and wife brought their past, their dreams, and their challenges. The son understood through his father's wisdom that a strong marriage required balance—respect for old traditions, but openness to new ways. His father had taught him that navigating this shared journey was about honouring the past while embracing change, and that the foundation of a family was built on mutual respect, love, and strength. As the son reflected on these lessons, he realised the importance of carrying these values forward in his own life.

Foundations of Your Legacy – 93

It is here, my son, you've stepped into the new,
Guarding old values while embracing what's true.
In this journey of life, you forge your own way,
Respecting all people, old and new, each day.

You carry the past with honour and pride,
Yet greet the future with arms open wide.
The balance you seek, where old meets the new,
Is where your true strength and wisdom come through.

In harmony's dance of tradition and change,
You find your own path, both steady and strange.
For in this blend, both steadfast and free,
Lies the foundation of your legacy.

Reflection 93: Foundations of Your Legacy

The son remembered his father's words about legacy and the importance of balancing the old with the new. His father had often spoken of the need to honour the past, to carry forward the values and lessons that had shaped him, but never to let them hold him back from embracing the future. The son understood that his father's guidance was about creating harmony between what had been and what was yet to come. By blending the wisdom of the past with the opportunities of the future, the son could build a legacy that was both strong and adaptable. In this balance, his father had shown him, lay the foundation of a life well-lived and a legacy that would endure.

Embracing the Night's Rest – 94

When late at night you lie awake,
With a restless mind that thoughts overtake,
Unable to sleep, as worries creep,
And the weight of the day runs deep.

Remember, my son, in those sleepless hours,
Your mind turns to tasks that still hold power.
Unfinished they are, and they'll linger and sway,
Until answers are found to clear the way.

These thoughts are the echoes of what's left undone,
A call to resolve them, one by one.
For peace will come when the tasks are through,
And the night will grant the rest that's due.

Reflection 94: Embracing the Night's Rest

The son often struggled with sleepless nights, when his mind raced with thoughts of unfinished tasks and unanswered questions. His father had once told him that these moments of restlessness were not to be feared but embraced. They were a sign that something important was calling for his attention, something unresolved that lingered in the quiet hours of the night. His father had advised him to use these moments as a time for reflection, to find the answers that would bring him peace. The son realised that by addressing these lingering tasks, he could find the rest he needed. His father's words reminded him that peace would come once the mind was clear, and sleep would follow when the day's burdens were laid to rest.

The Midnight Call – 95

Remember, my son, when midnight keeps you awake,
And sleep eludes you as new thoughts take shape.
These are tasks calling out, needing your care,
Unfinished and pressing, they linger in the air.

You weren't prepared for them, not in the light of day,
But in the quiet of night, they come out to play.
These moments, my son, are a dawn of their own,
Preparing you quietly before the real dawn is shown.

Embrace these hours, where the mind finds its way,
For they ready your heart for the challenges of day.
In this midnight stirring, there's a strength to be found,
Guiding you forward when morning comes 'round.

Reflection 95: The Midnight Call

The son had often found himself awake in the middle of the night, his mind filled with thoughts that had eluded him during the day. His father had once told him that the quiet of the night was a time when the mind could finally catch up to what the day had left undone. It was a time to listen to the tasks that called out for attention, not to fear them, but to embrace them. His father had explained that these midnight moments were a kind of preparation for the challenges ahead, a time when clarity could emerge before the dawn. The son understood that in these moments of quiet reflection, he could find the strength

Finding Peace in Unresolved Tasks – 96

For those, my son, who find rest elusive,
Either before midnight or as dawn approaches,
Know this: tasks linger, unresolved,
Some wait for resolution, others for insight evolved.

These lingering thoughts may confuse and collide,
As priorities shift and clarity hides.
Face them, my son, confront what's due,
For only through resolution can you find what's true.

Let not these shadows cloud your way,
Address them directly to clear the grey.
For in facing these tasks, both urgent and deep,
You'll find the path and the peace you seek.

Reflection 96: Finding Peace in Unresolved Tasks

The son often found himself lying awake at night, his mind crowded with unresolved thoughts. His father had told him that these lingering tasks, the ones that refuse to leave the corners of the mind, were not to be feared but faced head-on. His father had taught him that clarity and peace only come when the unresolved is addressed.

The son remembered that his father had emphasised how important it was to clear away the shadows of unresolved tasks, whether they were small or significant. By addressing them directly, the son could find the path to the peace he sought. His father's wisdom had always guided him through these moments of uncertainty, reminding him that peace followed clarity.

Son, understand this about money's flow,
It often arrives from places we don't know.
When it comes unexpectedly, keep it safe,
For it may not stay long, but quickly escape.

When planning your future, think ahead and strive,
To earn what you need to keep your goals alive.
Money earned with intention aligns with your plan,
So focus your efforts, and act with a clear span.

Be mindful of what comes your way,
But for your aspirations, let foresight lead the day.
Money is a tool, and you are its guide,
Use it wisely, with purpose by your side.

Reflection 97: Guiding Your Path with Money

The son recalled his father's lessons about money and its unpredictable nature. His father had often spoken of how money could come from unexpected places, but just as easily, it could slip away. The son had learned to treat financial windfalls with care, never assuming they would last without proper management.

His father had emphasised that planning ahead and earning money with clear intentions was the best way to ensure stability. By aligning his earnings with his goals, the son could build a secure foundation. His father's wisdom on treating money as a tool, rather than a goal in itself, helped him make thoughtful decisions, using it wisely to support his aspirations.

The World of Schools and Building Their Spirit – 98

Schools and colleges, where young minds are shaped,
In halls of learning, their futures are draped.
Children spend their days in pursuit of the best,
Competing and striving to stand out from the rest.

Some excel in subjects, mastering the art,
Others find their way in fields that set them apart.
But remember, my child, this academic stage,
Is just one world of learning, a single page.

The lessons here might seem to confound,
As family and school offer views so profound.
But in this world of knowledge and skill,
You must find your way, with your heart and your will.

Reflection 98: The World of Schools and
Building Their Spirit

The son remembered his father's advice about education, how the world of schools and colleges was only one stage in the broader journey of life. His father had explained that while academic success was important, it was not the only measure of growth.

His father had always encouraged him to find his own path amidst the knowledge and competition, to stay true to his values while navigating the demands of academic life. As the son reflected on his father's wisdom, he realised that the lessons learned in school were just the beginning. What mattered most was how he applied them with heart and determination in the real world.

Building Their Spirit – 99

In each young heart, a spirit resides,
A strength to face life's shifting tides.
The world may challenge, with trials untold,
But within you, my child is the courage to hold.

Though schools may test, and the world demands,
Remember, your worth lies in your own hands.
You are more than grades, more than the race,
Your spirit is strong, in every place.

Build your confidence, with each step you take,
For it's your journey, your path to make.
The lessons you learn, both inside and out,
Will shape your life, without a doubt.

So, stand tall, my child, with faith in your core,
Your spirit will guide you to so much more.
In every challenge, find the strength to rise,
For within you lies the power to touch the skies.

Reflection 99: Building Their Spirit

The son often thought of his father's words about inner strength. His father had always spoken of the spirit that lived within each of us, a quiet strength that could carry us through even the toughest challenges. His father had reminded him that grades and achievements, while important, were not the true measure of a person.

The son understood that his father had placed more value on character, resilience, and the ability to rise above life's demands. With each step he took, the son realized that it was his inner spirit that would guide him to success. His father's lessons on self-worth had taught him that real strength came from within, and with it, he could overcome anything.

The Breed of Fighters – 100

These are the breed that learn to fight,
Sharpening skills under the harshest light.
They share the knowledge to overtake,
In the race of life, no chances to forsake.

When defeat comes, they cannot bear,
But find new strength in the battles they dare.
The rules of the game are ever so clear,
Winning is all that they hold dear.

Some move like foxes, cunning and sly,
Others like lions, with a fierce, roaring cry.
They chase success with relentless pace,
Each victory sweet in this endless race.

But remember, my child, in this quest for might,
It's not just winning that defines the fight.
For in each battle, there's more to gain,
Lessons learned in loss, and strength in pain.

Reflection 100: The Breed of Fighters

The son remembered his father's stories of those who fought through life's challenges with determination. His father had always admired those who, like foxes or lions, pursued their goals with relentless energy. Winning was important to them, but his father had taught him that victory alone did not define success.

The son had learned from his father that each battle carried lessons—both in triumph and defeat. It was the strength built through loss and the wisdom gained in adversity that truly defined a fighter. As the son faced his own challenges, he held onto his father's belief that the real fight was not just in winning but in the growth that came from the journey.

The Quiet Victory – 101

Understand the rules of this game, my child,
Where victory isn't always loud or wild.
There's much to hide, much to bear,
In silence you stand, with thoughts laid bare.

Keeping quiet, letting others believe,
Uncertain if winning is what you'll achieve.
In this game, the lines aren't always clear,
Success might seem distant, but don't live in fear.

For strength lies not just in overt displays,
But in the quiet, patient, and subtle ways.
Master the art of holding your ground,
In silence, the truest victories are found.

Reflection 101: The Quiet Victory

The son often pondered his father's wisdom on silent victories. His father had taught him that not all victories were loud or celebrated. Some were won in silence through patience and persistence. His father had always said that strength wasn't always in showing power but in quietly holding one's ground.

The son realized that his father's lessons had taught him to navigate the unseen battles of life. He understood now that success didn't always need to be visible to others. True victory came in those moments when he stood firm, even when the world wasn't watching.

The Integrity of Victory – 102

You don't need to play the games they play,
When victories are snatched, fairness fades away.
Blaming the game, or changing the rules,
In a world where some take others for fools.

Understand, my child, that life's a game,
One, we all should strive to win with honour, not shame.
It's not about pulling others down,
But lifting yourself up without stealing a crown.

Play with integrity, with a heart that's true,
For in life's long game, it's not just about you.
Victory is sweetest when earned by the right,
Where all can rise and share in the light.

Reflection 102: The Integrity of Victory

The son recalled his father's strong words about fairness and integrity in life's competitive games. His father had always discouraged taking shortcuts or manipulating the rules to win, explaining that such victories were hollow. The son had learned that real success came from playing with honour, where the goal was not just to win but to win fairly.

His father had taught him that integrity was more important than achieving recognition at any cost. The son understood that lifting oneself up without pulling others down was the truest form of success. In a world where some were tempted to cheat, his father's lessons reminded him that the most rewarding victories were the ones earned through honest effort.

Careers begin where the heart finds its start,
In the warmth of family, where love plays a part.
Support and encouragement, like seeds well sown,
Build confidence and strength, where dreams are grown.

Listening to stories of struggles and fight,
Taking advice to guide through the night.
In the family's embrace, wisdom is shared,
Preparing for a world that often feels unprepared.

The external world offers paths to explore,
But with judgment and tests, it demands even more.
Yet the roots of your journey, strong and deep,
Are nurtured at home, where values you keep.

Reflection 103: Foundations of a Career

The son had often thought about his father's guidance on building a career. His father had always emphasised that while the external world would offer many opportunities, the true foundation of a successful career began at home, in the warmth of family support. The son had learned that love, encouragement, and wisdom from his family were like seeds that helped dreams take root and grow strong.

His father had reminded him that while the outside world would test him and challenge his values, it was the lessons learned at home that would sustain him. As the son ventured into his career, he carried with him the deep-rooted values instilled by his father, knowing they would guide him through whatever came his way.

The Silent Influence of Home – 104

The atmosphere at home, a silent force,
Can steer a career on its destined course.
But when undermining words or disappointment reigns,
Dreams may falter, caught in unseen chains.

Look at the close-knit family ties,
Sometimes so near, yet distant in their rise.
Bound by blood, yet growth held back,
By an environment that lacks what others might lack.

Support is more than just being there,
It's fostering dreams with genuine care.
For careers can flourish or wither away,
In the home where the seeds of success lay.

Reflection 104: The Silent Influence of Home

The son remembered his father's observations about how the atmosphere at home could quietly shape or hinder one's future. His father had always pointed out that while family ties were important, they could sometimes hold one back if the environment wasn't nurturing enough. The son had learned that genuine support went beyond just being physically present; it involved actively fostering dreams and offering encouragement.

His father had warned that negative or undermining words at home could chain one's aspirations in subtle ways. As the son reflected on his father's wisdom, he realised how crucial it was to create a positive and supportive environment for growth. His father's insights helped him understand the powerful influence a home could have on a person's success.

In the journey of career, choose with care,
The people who'll guide you beyond compare.
Seek mentors who see your dreams unfold,
With wisdom and support, both brave and bold.

Align with those who share your core values tight,
With ethics and integrity shining bright.
Their paths, aligned with yours, should weave,
In a tapestry of success, you both believe.

Reflection 105: Choosing Mentors and Values

The son had often sought his father's advice on finding the right mentors in his career. His father had told him that choosing a mentor was more than just finding someone successful—it was about aligning with someone who shared his values. His father had emphasised that a true mentor was someone who not only offered wisdom and support but also walked a path of integrity and ethics.

The son learned that by choosing mentors who believed in his dreams and held the same core values, their journeys would weave together toward shared success. His father's wisdom reminded him to seek guidance from those who could both challenge and uplift him, ensuring that his growth would be meaningful and aligned with his principles.

Embracing Diversity and Collaboration – 106

Embrace the diversity of their thought and view,
For new perspectives spark ideas anew.
Let their varied skills and backgrounds blend,
To foster growth that knows no end.

Choose collaborators who lift, not compete,
Who celebrate your triumphs and make you complete.
In mutual support, find your career's grace,
Where success is shared in every embrace.

Reflection 106: Embracing Diversity and Collaboration

The son had often heard his father speak about the importance of collaboration and diversity in work and life. His father had taught him that by embracing different perspectives, new ideas could spark and grow. The son had learned that true success wasn't found in competing with others but in choosing collaborators who supported each other's goals.

His father's wisdom had guided him to understand that when people from different backgrounds and skills came together, their collective strength could accomplish great things. The son realised that by working with those who uplifted him, he could foster an environment of growth, where success was shared and celebrated.

Look for those who inspire you to learn and grow,
Challenging you to reach beyond what you know.
With a thirst for knowledge that never fades,
They'll guide you through life's ever-changing shades.

Value emotional intelligence in their art,
Empathy and communication from the start.
In complex dynamics, let them be your guide,
Navigating relationships with care and pride.

Select those with a vision that's long and true,
Building foundations strong for success to ensue.
For in their foresight, patience, and strategic plan,
Lies the path to a career where dreams can expand.

Reflection 107: Growth, Emotional Intelligence, and Vision

The son remembered how his father had often spoken of the qualities to seek in others, especially mentors and leaders. His father had told him to look for those who could challenge him to grow, who never stopped learning themselves. The son had learned that emotional intelligence—empathy, communication, and understanding—was as important as knowledge when navigating complex relationships.

His father had emphasised the importance of aligning with people who had long-term vision, patience, and a strategic plan. By surrounding himself with such individuals, the son knew he would be guided along a path that not only supported his dreams but also helped him build something lasting and meaningful.

The Celestial Influence – 108

In the vast cosmic dance, each planet plays,
Much like the roles in our lives' complex maze.
Mercury, swift, with a quicksilver grace,
Like friends who bring energy to our space.

Venus, glowing with a tender light,
Reflects the warmth of our loved ones' might.
Earth, our constant, cradles life's embrace,
Mirrors the care of family's grace.

Mars, bold and fierce in its fiery hue,
Echoes the elders, whose strength guides us through.
Jupiter, with its mighty, swirling bands,
Represents the support from guiding hands.

Saturn, with rings that mark its domain,
Reflects the lessons learned through joy and pain.
Uranus, with a tilt and a subtle shift,
Signifies the change that brings a needed lift.

Neptune, deep in its mysterious sea,
Speaks to the introspection we all need to be.
And Pluto, distant, with its quiet claim,
Reminds us of memories that never wane.

Each planet, like those in our earthly sphere,
Influences our lives, both far and near.
In their cosmic roles, we see our own,
Understanding their impact as we journey on.

Reflection 108: The Celestial Influence

The son reflected on the cosmic analogies his father had often shared. His father had compared the people and influences in life to the planets in their grand dance, each with its unique traits. Mercury was like the friend who energized life with quick movement and communication, while Venus embodied the warmth and love that family and close relationships provided.

His father had taught him that each person around him played a role in shaping his journey, much like the planets influencing their celestial paths. By understanding these influences and their impact, the son could navigate his own life with more clarity, knowing that just like the planets, the people around him were part of the vast interconnected web of his life.

Relationships Retrograde – 109

In the celestial realm, planets drift and sway,
Retrograde phases mark a curious display.
Their usual paths seem to falter and bend,
Mirroring the phases our relationships spend.

When Mercury's retrograde brings confusion and strain,
So too can miscommunications create similar pain.
In friendships and bonds, the words misalign,
Leading to moments where understanding's hard to define.

Venus in retrograde clouds love's gentle light,
Echoes how affection can falter in sight.
Romantic ties may struggle and strain,
Yet these phases reveal deeper truths to gain.

Saturn's backward motion stirs old fears and tests,
Reflecting how family conflicts manifest.
Lessons from the past resurface anew,
Challenging us to heal and to renew.

Mars retrogrades bring conflicts, slow and steep,
Similar to arguments that stir from the deep.
Energy shifts and passions run high,
Demanding patience as tempers may fly.

As planets retrograde and their influence shifts,
So do our bonds through relational rifts.
In these phases, though turbulent and tense,
We find growth and clarity, often immense.

Reflection 109: Relationships Retrograde

The son remembered his father's wisdom about the shifting dynamics of relationships, comparing them to the retrograde movements of planets. His father had explained that just as planets appear to move backward during retrograde, so too do relationships sometimes falter, causing confusion and strain. The son had learned that during these periods, communication often broke down, and misunderstandings could cloud even the closest bonds.

His father had taught him that these phases were not to be feared, but embraced as opportunities for growth. Just as retrogrades reveal hidden truths in the cosmos, relationship struggles reveal deeper lessons about patience, resilience, and understanding. Through his father's words, the son understood that even in turbulent times, there was immense clarity and growth to be found.

The Unsaid Faiths – 110

Son, they say Pluto may not be a planet clear,
Yet, in the cosmic dance, its presence remains near.
So too are people around us, not always defined,
Not by blood or relation, but by the ties that bind.

In the realm of the unsaid, where words go astray,
We may not know where these connections lay.
In those silent moments and the things left unspoken,
Lies a hidden faith that remains unbroken.

For in these unsaid times, and in words left unsaid,
There exists a trust that silently spreads.
Like Pluto's orbit, mysterious and grand,
These unseen bonds offer a guiding hand.

They may not fit neatly into roles we know,
Yet their presence in our lives continues to grow.
In the quiet and the void where definitions fall,
Invisible faiths are present, guiding us all.

Reflection 110: The Unsaid Faiths

The son thought about his father's reflections on the unseen bonds between people, those connections that were not always easy to define. His father had often spoken of these "unsaid faiths," likening them to Pluto's mysterious presence in the cosmos. Just as Pluto's influence persisted despite its distant orbit, so too did the silent trust between individuals.

His father had taught him that these quiet connections, though unspoken, were powerful and enduring. The son realised that some relationships, though not bound by blood or formal ties, carried a deep and abiding trust. His father's wisdom reminded him that these unsaid faiths guided him through life's uncertainties, offering a subtle yet strong support when it was needed most.

The Field of Perspectives – 111

When choosing whom to share your thoughts and views,
Consider their place in the field they choose.
In this diverse terrain, people play varied roles,
Each at a different stage, with unique goals.

Some are just planting, their ideas take root,
While others are watering, tending their pursuit.
Then come the harvesters, with knowledge well-earned,
Their insights are ripe, from lessons discerned.

Each phase brings wisdom, unique and profound,
In this field of perspectives, true growth is found.
Honour the stages, for each has its worth,
Helping you navigate your own path on earth.

Reflection 111: The Field of Perspectives

The son remembered how his father had often spoken about the different stages of growth that people experience, both in life and in their understanding. His father had explained that everyone was in a different place, some just beginning to plant the seeds of their ideas, while others were nurturing those ideas into something more substantial.

The son had learned to respect the perspectives of those at every stage—whether they were starting out or seasoned experts. His father's wisdom had taught him to listen carefully to the insights of others, knowing that each person's journey brought its own value. The son understood that by honouring these different phases, he could grow in his own path, enriched by the perspectives of those around him.

The Stage You're In – 112

In the journey of growth, it's wise to discern,
Which stage you're in, and the lessons to learn.
Are you just budding, with fresh ideas to sprout,
Or are you harvesting, with knowledge throughout?

If you're in the budding phase, with dreams taking flight,
Seek out a mentor to help guide your light.
Their wisdom will nurture the seeds you have sown,
And help you grow stronger as you make your own.

If you're in the harvesting stage, with insights so clear,
Share your knowledge widely, and let others draw near.
For even when seasoned, there's more to learn,
In the ever-turning cycles, there's growth to discern.

Reflection 112: The Stage You're In

The son often recalled his father's advice about being mindful of the stage he was in. His father had explained that life's journey was one of constant growth, and understanding where you stood on that path was essential for knowing how to move forward. Whether at the start, when dreams were just budding, or later, when experience had been harvested, each stage offered valuable lessons.

His father had emphasised the importance of seeking guidance when new ideas were forming and sharing wisdom when it was well-earned. The son understood that growth wasn't linear but cyclical, and even in moments of mastery, there was always room to learn more. His father's wisdom helped him navigate life's cycles with clarity and purpose.

The Path to Inner Freedom - 113

When people fight for rights and freedom,
Believing someone holds their kingdom,
They often think it's with a foe,
And that they must wrest it to be free, you know.

But, son, no one can chain your soul,
No one can grant you freedom whole.
It's not something given or taken away,
But a choice you make each and every day.

The struggle isn't with an external hand,
But with the mind where doubts take a stand.
The moment you decide to let them go,
You'll find your spirit free to grow.

Don't be deceived by the battles outside,
True freedom's where your heart does abide.
It's not in conflicts, nor in strife,
But in your soul, where freedom comes to life.

Reflection 113: The Path to Inner Freedom

As the son reflected on his father's words about freedom, he began to grasp the deeper truth behind the struggle for rights and liberation. His father had always emphasised that true freedom is not something that can be granted by others or taken away by circumstances. Instead, it resides within each individual, waiting to be discovered and embraced.

The son remembered his father's insistence that while many perceive their battles as external conflicts with foes or systems, the most significant struggle lies within. It is in the mind, where doubts and fears can imprison the spirit, that the fight for freedom truly takes place. His father taught him that the moment one chooses to release these mental chains, the path to growth and self-realisation opens wide.

In pondering these lessons, the son recognised that the essence of freedom is about making daily choices that reflect one's values and desires. It is not defined by external approval or societal norms but by the authenticity of one's heart and soul. With this understanding, he felt a renewed sense of empowerment, ready to face the world and his own inner challenges with clarity and strength.

The Journey Beyond – 114

In the silence that followed your final breath,
A quiet journey began beyond death.
To a place where peace and light reside,
Where you walk now with no need to hide.

The struggles of life have fallen away,
As you travel to realms where spirits stay.
Greeted by those who left before,
Their love surrounds you forevermore.

Each step you take in the light's embrace,
Brings you closer to truth, and to grace.
No more pain, no more burdens, no strife,
Just the endless beauty of eternal life.

Do you see us from your place on high?
Do our thoughts reach you where angels fly?
We miss you here, your voice, your touch,
But we trust in the love that binds us so much.

As you journey on in heaven's light,
May your soul find peace, your heart take flight.
We carry your love in all that we do,
Knowing one day, we'll journey there too.

Reflection 114: The Journey Beyond

The son reflected on his father's passing, imagining the peaceful journey his father must now be on. His father had always spoken of life beyond this world, where the burdens of daily struggles would fall away, replaced by the light of truth and grace. The son found comfort in the thought that his father had been welcomed by those who had gone before, surrounded by love and peace.

Though the son missed his father deeply, he trusted in the love that continued to bind them. His father's teachings about life, love, and eternity had prepared him to understand that while the physical presence was gone, the bond between them would never fade. As the son carried on, he knew that one day, they would meet again on this new journey, guided by the love that had always connected them.

Father: Sri Rama Murthy
Mother: Santha
Elder Brother: Vinay Kumar
Sister: Usha
Second Brother: Nirmal Kumar
Fourth Gen Kids: Sri Nand and Druv
Me: Vijay Kumar

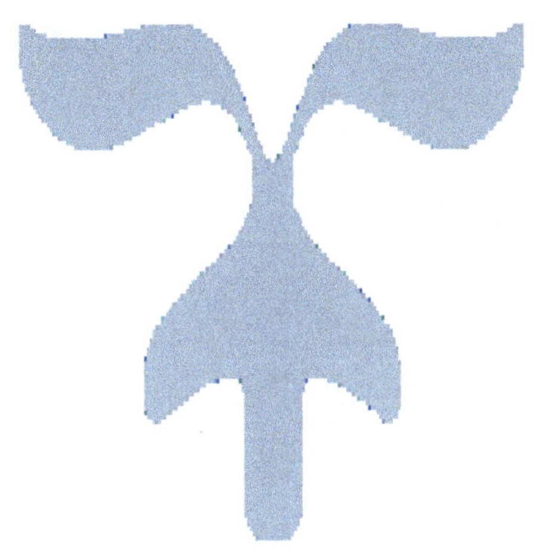